Seed of Dragons

Surviving an Empire Undone

by Billy Ironcrane

For me Buddy

Something To

Relax your mind.

R

For permissions contact:

www.ironcrane.com/html/contactus.html

Published by:
Mc Cabe and Associates
Tacoma, WA.

Illustrated by Renee Knarreborg
Cover Design Mc Cabe and Associates
Cover image by Bobbi Youtcheff "Fall at Point Defiance"
Author Photo by Doug Goodman

ISBN-13: 978-1-7324154-3-0
Library of Congress Control Number: 2019910845

To Storytellers everywhere

Truth will not be buried;
so long as you plow your craft.

Contents

Illustrations

Seed
of
Dragons

Introduction

We bring you two stories...Within, you'll glimpse into the lives of two heroes. They don't think of themselves as such, not at these points in their lives anyway. They're just trying to be who they know they are, in a world which seeks to compel otherwise. It's here their respective histories begin. You'll see in each instance how they push through uncertainty and strive to achieve their full potential, no matter the odds against. You'll witness how life shapes, pushes and delivers each onto his respective heroic journey. Who can say where the two will end up, or how they will fare. One thing for sure, in the end, they will have been true to themselves, just as they were in their early beginnings, forever unshakable in the face of overwhelming threat. In these accounts and others yet to come, we'll share with you what we know, and together, we'll wish only the best for them, realizing all the while, nothing is guaranteed.

You should know this. All of the happenings within follow the collapse of the Han dynasty, considered by many to have been the golden era of Chinese history. After nearly four centuries of exemplary rule, the dynasty became corrupted and, expectations aside, disintegrated upon itself from within. As this unfolded, three great leaders emerged to contend for power and the divine right to re-establish the once empire. At first, they hoped to preserve the Mandate of Heaven and the appearance of continuity from the traditional Han. In the end, they had no choice but to make do without.

The stories of those times are many and varied, and have been dutifully preserved for our benefit in the records of historians, but more elegantly in the carefully woven efforts of artists, poets and writers, the great interpreters of reality. Foremost among their works is *Romance of the Three Kingdoms*[1], by the 14th century playwright Luo Guanzhong. His account addresses the period immediately post Han, lasting approximately five generations, where bedlam reigned, and what remained of the once glorious empire fell to three contentious warring kingdoms.

Culminating that troubled period, we know the empire eventually came briefly under one rule. Then in a quick moment, fragmented completely: hopelessly gyrating uncontrollably for hundreds of years and delivering the population to disunity, carnage, starvation, disease, indenture and destitution.

---

[1] There are a number of commendable translations available. Among my favorites is: Luo, Guanzhong, and Moss Roberts. *Three Kingdoms: a Historical Novel; Complete and Unabridged.* Berkeley: Univ. of California Press, 2005. Print.

It is then when our current stories begin and take their root. Join us as we connect the diverse links strewn about the landscape of time and events, looking to see if somehow they might ever meld into a coherent whole, capable of guiding us through ages of uncertainty, and giving hope for the future. Our future.

Background

Story one begins with two friends on the side of a frozen
mountain, resting in their snow cave after a long day's
upward trek. While warming and recovering strength, they
chat idly. As might happen with any of us in like
circumstance, their banter veers into the mysteries of life and
the nature of reality and existence. This leads the elder,
Abbot Shi-Hui Ke, to recount an incident from his
childhood. With him is Bao Ling, a falsely accused fugitive
from the east. Shi-Hui Ke has granted him sanctuary in a
remote western monastery servicing the oppressed Shu
mountain tribes. He commences with recollections of himself
as a boy accompanying his master and the tribal elders on a
trip to market. Soon enough, the narrative takes on a life of
its own. Through what unfolds, we discover in our own
innocence the vast uncertainties of troubled times, and the
weighty consequences of even the most subtle of decisions.
"Hui," that's how we shall call him, recalls from his distant
memories the heroic deeds of his teacher, and a motley
assortment of new friends and allies gathered from within
the folds of uncertainty and hopelessness. But it is Hui, as a

young boy on whom everything pivots and by story's end you will agree he is marked for greatness, and for trials.

In the second account, set many years later, you will make more formal acquaintance with Bao Ling, of whom in time we shall say much more. Bao Ling, now as an older and life-wizened man, finds himself forced by necessity to revisit with his son the particulars of his past. In some ways, Bao Ling is every person, just like you, just like me. He emerges as a humble peasant, no different than his forbears, good folk and relations who preceded him in what came to be called Ling village. There his ancestors lived for as long as anyone can remember. A kind and friendly people dedicated to their land, their traditions, and their ways, possessing little but themselves, the essentials of life, and contentment. You would think they'd be ignored and overlooked as the fates of empires swirled in vicious currents about them. But as is so common with those deemed helpless, they are not. It is said conflict, chaos and strife tend to drift like plagues, seemingly lifted by ill winds and propelled by misguided minds to places where they have no purpose or right to be. Those same ill winds drive the flow of events which turn to envelop both heroes.

You'll see how both, though nurtured in different worlds, were carefully steeped from childhood in self reliance and in fending for themselves. It's often that way with these kinds of people. They're never so primitive or base as some would have you imagine. Shi-Hui Ke had been guided by Master Li. For Bao Ling, it was He Ling, his paternal grandfather. You'll marvel at the extent to which Bao Ling strives to hone and polish his skills, ever attuned to the mantra imparted by his grandfather, "We come from a family anointed to be the final line against oppression. We will not shirk our fate!"

Though their paths have merged for a moment on the frozen slopes, these two recitations stand many years apart, during which much has passed for each of them: from where it all started, and from where they once sat together as friends one snowy evening. Despite all unlikelihood, benign fortune ordained for the two heroes to somehow meet and to partner in the ultimate struggle to preserve their respective people and their ways, an undertaking which in the end, takes on cosmic proportions. In due time, we'll tell of their deeds, and those of many others, leaving no uncertainty as to what defines the nature of highest character.

These tales are fantasies, born first from my dreams, supplemented by myth, and at times, loosely, by history, personal experience, and lessons from a noble teacher. Wherever possible, I have avoided letting what some would insist to be fact, getting in the way of a good yarn. The heart of the matter is in the telling. Look there for what you need, then find your own truth.

Middle Kingdom

Empire Adrift

Book 1

Master Li Confronts the Wei

The Thought Cuts

The day grew late for Abbot Hui and Bao Ling. The air along the ridge cooled markedly with the night winds beginning their race to the valleys below. Once iced, the alpine ridges became treacherous. The pair had made good early progress on the ascent. Now, challenged by the change in conditions and depleted from the day's exertions, their upward steps required utmost care and attention.

Even with the iron feet and their spiked bottoms, every step had to be carefully set and placed. A premature lean on a footstep not yet anchored meant an abrupt drop down an icy slope followed by frantic efforts to drive a spike, blade or rod into the skimming-by sheen which by then felt no different than polished stone.

Among the Shu people, even experienced climbers chilled at the prospect. Sitting around campfires they commonly made light of their misadventures and unanticipated crash landings, taking turns to show and compare scars. This usually quieted when someone recalled memories of friends not so lucky or skilled, or who simply disappeared, leaving only the finger trail of their timid blade's panicked scratch and peck, pointing wistfully to the crevasse or chasm where they met their ends.

As the sun lowered in the west, the two agreed to set camp just below the top notch of a horse hoof ravine descending from the high ridge to their front. Once there, the cold pressed hard upon them. They said nothing, saving their body heat and their energy for the task of punching a hole and digging an ice cave into the slope. They placed the finishing touches just as the sun dipped over the western ridges. Inside, they cut shelves where they could lay and rest. For warmth, two candles were placed. From within, where the ambient candlelight reached timidly beyond the entry hole, they saw it had begun to snow. Large flakes blew furiously over the newly minted ice beneath. They remained silent. Nobody really wants idle chatter when bodies tremor for want of warmth. Though light and heat from candles diminish with thin air at altitude, both knew there would be enough to soon bring comfort to the interior. Only then could their bodies relax. Once shivering abated, they would eat and prepare for sleep. There would be no fire. Fuel was too heavy and dear a commodity to pack and carry, except for some oiled charcoal and dung chips kept only for emergencies. Their meal of fish and dried berries with some sticky rice lightened their spirits and added to the stores of energy available to warm them. By then, their eyes had adjusted to the light of the candles and they settled comfortably.

"Bao Ling, have you ever heard the expression 'The thought cuts'?"

Bao Ling folded himself for comfort over a fur placed on the icy shelf. His pack, now backstop, supported his upper body, his reddened face reflected glow from the adjacent candle. He had no idea where this question would lead, or even if he wanted to go there. He had been enjoying the silence, the white flakes racing among the shadows outside, and the weighted cold air, now beginning to roar its downhill descent. One could almost hear a mountain breathing at times like this.

"Why are you asking that?"

"No particular reason," Hui answered, "Just something to talk about and idle the time before we sleep. How about I start by telling you what I know, then we can compare experiences. Master Li Fung first said it to me long ago, as did some of the other elders when I studied the fighting arts in my youth. It's not the same thing as, but it bears some relation to what happens when I use the thought arrow[2]."

"Ah, thought arrow! That remarkable demonstration you gave when the tiger nearly had Zhi Mei, prompting her to chastise we needn't have come to her rescue?"

"Yeah, seems like a good name, don't you think? I postulate it as an arrow and somehow that determines its character. I suspect by the way, protests aside, she appreciated our showing up when we did and even our honest efforts."

---

[2] Bao Ling had already seen Abbot Hui's remarkable skill using concentrated thought, weapon like, to deter a stalking tiger. The full account is presented elsewhere.

He went on, "In my youth, our people moved about constantly. Survival demanded it. Forced to be nomads in our own territory, the hills spilled over with intruders. Great rewards and riches awaited whichever ambitious warlords could conquer the Shu ranges and unravel the secrets of their many trails and arteries. As is the case even now, all sought quick passage to the west, and that required subjugation of the natives. Most who tried to plumb the depths of that well, in due time, found it dry indeed. Rare are those who can tame dragons. Only one person ever unlocked the secrets of our ranges in their entirety. He had been our beloved friend and benefactor. We still may not want to believe it, but regrettably, we all know Zhuge Liang has passed on. Out of respect for him, the Shu tribes weren't about to give all we had learned to a horde of conniving bastards.

The unending threats persisted, and the constant need to run at a moment's notice required we master the necessary survival skills and fighting arts. That continues to this day. You've already witnessed this in the monks, and in your two young proteges. As a youth, my own tutelage fell to the charge of Master Li Fung, whom you already know."

"Yes, a greatly skilled master."

"Even more than you can imagine. Well, we came to him as young children, so critical had the demands of those times become. His thought had always been, 'The younger, the better. The younger body remains pliable, the mind within nimble and quick.' This played true as I'm sure you know. Even as children, many of us had to think and fight for our lives. Ultimately, we proved one thing certain. Li Fung's teachings weren't wasted.

"You see, even now he believes in the ascendance of mind over matter. I've watched what you do. You know what I'm talking about. Starting from somewhere inside, there exists a profound center from where we manifest our essential beings and our true natures. That center links us to the great void, and to each other. What we think to be ourselves stands between, like a big brazen rock. Master Laozi spoke of this in his Tao. Master Li certainly had a handle on it. Regretfully, despite my years I am still but a novice, though always learning. At times the process can be punishingly slow, but I can declare to you I am starting to make progress. Very slow progress."

They both laughed at this, each knowing well his personal struggles with life and distraction.

Bao Ling smiled quietly at Hui's humility. Though friends for only a short time, he already knew Hui to be a giant among men, with considerable skills and great responsibilities, serving purposes which hinted at cosmic significance, but of which they never spoke.

Hui continued, "Master Li summed it up in three words, 'The thought cuts.' That's a deep well of course, and as children, for us it meant nothing though he repeated it often. No matter. Eventually it became clear. He believed action honed character. Slowly, like shaping precious jade. You see, as we practiced in the beginning, he had us execute countless repetitions ... you've probably heard the rule of ten thousand?"

"Yes, 10,000 repetitions. You don't truly know anything until you've done it 10,000 times. If your goal is mastery of a new skill, you will only achieve it with 10,000 repetitions. Interesting, we too thought of it as mind over matter."

Ownership

"Well, we did the repetitions, and it worked. But more remarkable was this. We did learn what we practiced; but what we learned grew further into something far beyond what we expected. Within the very core of our movement, we found something new and alive. No exaggeration, it felt like a snake slithering about. I'm talking about a tactile sensation, a feeling and sense very immediate, intimate, as straightforward and evident as our own heartbeats. Li Fung told us we were experiencing the worm of our chi stirring in its cocoon. He explained it could manifest in many ways, depending on the engagement and the use, sometimes like a rush of water, or the feeling of a pot boiling in our abdomen, perhaps a wave rising and falling within, or even like a snake ascending from the base of our spines to our heads.

"Frankly, it frightened us. This is the truth Bao Ling. At times it felt like some other being moved and shifted about. Imagine that. Inside our very bodies it was almost like something had taken lodging and now decided on its own to re-arrange the furniture and contents, doubtless suiting its own fancies."

Bao Ling responded, "Yes, I know of those sensations."

"Do you? Good! I'm reassured. You won't think I'm a loon if I continue. We were yet children. Granted we knew the seriousness of what we were doing, and what was expected of us, but these experiences were unnerving, especially given our superstitions and the fear defining the times."

"Superstitions?"

"Surely you know what I mean. You've likely seen it yourself. Ghosts behind every rock, ghouls flickering in the shadows at night, curses issued by jealous neighbors damming one's crops, neglected gods shedding tears and flooding villages. Does it ever stop?"

Bao Ling nodded, "True, I have seen these things, and have at times fallen prey to their so convenient enchantments. In the lowland villages, of necessity we found our awareness centered on life's immediate demands. It's the same with your people isn't it? Right there sits the battle line, starting with dawn, ending with nightfall. Pay attention to what confronts you in the moment. Still, many find it impossible to resist peering further outward into the shadows and attributing all which befalls them to those unknowns seated just beyond the common view. I confess I've even found comfort at times doing likewise, blaming whatever was out there for my own misfortunes and losses. Had you known me then you might even have come upon me howling in rage toward some remote expanse cursing who or whatever hijacked the strings to my life and destiny."

"Did it work?"

"Yes, like holding a bronze mirror to my own face. 'Here lies the true culprit,' a voice from within my own head would whisper."

Hui laughed, "Guilty! It's about ownership, isn't it? Indeed! You do know how it is. For the same reasons, in the temple, many come to seek peace and enlightenment. They look outside themselves for someone to tell them to look within."

"Like a change of clothes, I suppose? Get out of the earthly rags, put on the celestial saffron. See what happens. Hope for the best. Can't get worse."

"True, for some it's just like that. Not for the Buddha though, not for Laozi, or any of the other sages. They started by taking ownership, and once there, understood the full reach and import of their actions through all dimensions."

Bao Ling glanced at his friend, "At some point, I can't say exactly when, I stopped begging the gods for protection, or food, or warmth, or happiness and success. It occurred to me everyone had been doing that very thing all along, likely from the very first of us. Fact is it's hard to think of anyone who doesn't. If they were even there, the gods I mean, how boring it would be for them to hear that constant and ever droning litany of pleas and self serving requests from those below. Is it any wonder they would choose not to intervene while we systematically destroy ourselves? 'CAN WE HAVE SOME QUIET PLEASE!!!' is what they would yell back to our pleadings. In fact it's what they give us ... their silence, but we don't seem to have ears for that kind of stuff. It's what makes us free, isn't it?"

"Then you believe in nothing?"

"There's no easy answer for that. Whether I admit it or not, I believe in something sure enough to fight for it unceasingly. If not, I would have resigned to accept, perhaps welcome the first blade that came my way in the hands of an enemy intent on finishing me. But to define that something is not so easy. Self preservation? My people? Righteousness? The gift of life? It's more complicated than that. All seem to have become lost in the jumbled mix of reality and my relentless urge to continue. But for what? Who can say at this point? You know as well as I, we could both be gone tomorrow. Still, even in the midst of this quagmire, I look about, I see life everywhere, and marvel always at the many wonders, and the beauty. Could it be that life propels itself from within? Aware? When I speak with it, or relate to it without intruding or begging for favors, it seems to listen, and at times to reach my way. Not always, but enough to keep me motivated, and involved. Like an assuring old friend, not the gods, mind you, but life simply affirming itself. A favor to me perhaps, so that I don't give it up readily. I see it in the rocks, the dust, the wind, on the tips of eagle's wings and the teeth of wild dogs. I even see it in you, as we sit here now in the candlelight, just there behind the sheen on the surface of your eyes, a great mystery. 'Is that you?' I want to ask; almost expecting a primal creator's voice to spring from the great void and through you answer 'Damn! You have found me out!' "

Abbot Hui smiled warmly, "I like that Bao Ling. I might have said the same to you."

The two friends smiled at one another in silence. The mountain could be heard breathing more loudly outside, almost giving the impression of a curious giant's eye peeking in through the opening.

Abbot Shi-Hui Ke
"Then you believe in nothing?"

Hui Tells of Master Li

They sat and listened in silence, and at least once, both looked to the opening, almost expecting a presence to announce itself. Then, recognizing what had happened, each laughed self consciously, Abbot Hui finally shaking his head and murmuring, "Ghouls flickering in the shadows, such convenient enchantments."

Eventually, Bao Ling looked to his friend, "So … the thought cuts? What about it?"

Hui nodded, grateful for the return to topic. "Yes, the thought cuts. As the development of our skills continued, Master Li repeatedly cautioned when we worked with one another, 'Lads, remember to be careful, the thought can cut!' "

"At first, we had no clue. Judging by the punishment we were taking from each other, it became clear our skills had matured. If our practice became too robust, he would soon enough caution us about the thought cutting, so as to rein us in. We would ask him to explain, he'd tell us never mind, we needed to toughen first, just be careful. Explanations would come in due time."

"That's it?"

"Yes, until one occasion when we young students tagged along with Master Li and the village elders on a trading trip to the town Fortune's Gateway."

"I know the place."

"This was long ago, before you knew it, much different then. A thriving center in the middle of nowhere, connecting the east to the distant lands of the west. Due to lucky circumstance, it had become quite autonomous and wealthy. Far from the greedy reach of the many royal courts, it grew proud and self sufficient with commitment to equity in all undertakings, so long as fair profit might be gained.

"We pretty obviously were a bunch of mountain people. Our dress made that clear. The merchants had done business with us for generations, and knew us to be reliable and honest. They also knew, and pitied how we constantly faced threats from others hoping to dominate the Shu roads and our lands. No ill feelings existed between us and the locals. On this occasion however, we saw envoys from Wei[3],

---

[3] Wei. Name given to the eastern kingdom, yet another entity aspiring to empire. Though dominating the east, constant warfare had depleted their forces and resources. To survive and flourish, they looked westward for new wealth and replenishment, pushing into the Shu ranges and beyond. That meant they had to deal with or be rid of the Shu people.

our mortal enemies. Obviously, they were hoping to set the town against us. The skirmishes in the mountains had been tough on their forces, just as they had been on us. This new Wei vanguard planned to leverage the complicity of the town, using a combination of intimidation against the promise of reward and prosperity. They were hawking the argument how it would be best for townsfolk to come into the fold now, rather than wait for the Wei legions to spill from the Shu mountains and swallow them whole without recompense or recourse. Forming an alliance now would spare them from uncertainty and ensure their futures as comrades and partners. They would have status as honored friends, and respected voices. That same day, in the heart of town center, Wei criers were heralding their victories in the mountains, and predicting their legion's certain arrival before winter. If one could believe them, it didn't look good for us.

"We knew what they were saying to be a fabrication. I'm not sure the representatives from Wei knew the truth themselves. Often, they had only what they'd been told, and repeated what they'd been ordered to say. That's the nature of deception; it reaches deep from behind you and above you; pushing and weighing upon you until it becomes entrenched as your reality. Planting itself deeply, it steals even into your very thoughts and strongest beliefs. Then of course, you are sent to infect others.

"The elders in the party grew concerned, wanting nothing more than for us to be out of peril once trade and business finalized. The risks were too evident; we had no intention of becoming helpless prey, or of getting slaughtered needlessly. To the obvious consternation of his fellows, Li Fung insisted someone needed to correct the falsehoods being propagated, lest the good townsfolk be deceived and their goodwill lost. He knew already how losing commercial portals like Fortune's Gateway would cripple the western tribes in their ongoing struggles. That was after all Wei's hope and intent, indeed the very reason for their coming. Why not engage diplomacy to lessen the spilled blood of their troops?

"The elders told Li Fung to let it go, the time was not right, which only made him more adamant. He told them, 'No Problem! I can handle this.' and insisted the elders and our traders proceed home without him, arguing he didn't need their help anyway. I stood shocked when they agreed. Even for a child, there were no mysteries here. This was serious stuff!

"Master Li simply stared, face sullen and stern. Like one gazing to his own death emerging before him. Not much more could be said by anyone. He would waste no further time or argument over it. They knew where he stood. What one chose to undertake on his or her own deserved respect. We're like that you know. Again, it's about ownership, and giving it its due. On parting, they all took Li Fung by the hand, each tribesman individually. I witnessed in disbelief as they passed and bowed as though to a Buddha showing proper respect on his feast day. Only here, it looked too much like a funeral. Though a child, I could feel within me the dragon fire of mounting rage. They then hurriedly re-grouped, pushing quickly toward the nearest hills, looking for quick safety and refuge, not trusting the Wei were not already en route. Afterward, I learned that on taking his hand, each had whispered, 'I will avenge your death' making what they deemed to be a final pledge of fraternity. I can still hear Li Fung thanking them, and bowing quietly in respect as they parted. He bore no ill will, understanding they would all have their own duty and call to sacrifice in time, ensuring the survival of our people. He had firm faith each would do just as he had chosen to do, when their own moments came.

"Only I remained, but now stealthily hidden behind a boulder, taking all of it in. I couldn't believe what I thought I saw. Though not understanding the particulars, I made my own decision. I abandoned the entourage, and followed after Master Li. They saw and called for me to return, but it was too late. I moved away all the more quickly. I turned to them and yelled perhaps less respectfully than I should have, 'Child or not, I leave no friend, or teacher behind.' I did that to chastise and admonish them, not mature enough to know the great weight of responsibility and shame precariously balanced upon their shoulders. Years later, when my own mishap[4] occurred, I was reminded of this by those who came to my rescue. I told them to leave me, and to save their own skins. They used my own words against me, 'We leave no friend, or teacher behind,' causing me to wonder and reflect over the way words can span great time and distance, and somehow gather their own power along the way. Someday I must seek Zhi Mei's[5] insight on this.

---

[4] Shi-Hui Ke, while still a mountain warrior, had been ambushed and captured by a group of Wei mercenaries. Knowing his skill with the bow, they cut off his left thumb. Gangrene set in and the arm could not be saved. Only in the aftermath of this ordeal did he elect to enter the monastery.
[5] Zhi Mei - Bao Ling's traveling partner, and poetess supreme.

"As I raced away from the group, some were ordered to retrieve me, but I was too quick and clever. I left the road and before long, had them running in circles. To my dismay, I saw Li Fung walking more briskly back toward town, focusing only on what lay before him. I feared I might lose him. Might he have been pretending not to notice my little game with the pursuers? At some point, in exasperation, they gave it up; leaving me to share whatever might befall Li Fung. When I finally stood free, I raced toward the shadow in the distance, hoping to close the gap. As I neared, Master Li lent an ear to the sound of my approach. Without even turning, he called, 'Is that you, little Shi-Hui Ke?' "

Bao Ling could only smile at this. He too had known masters. It seemed nothing could escape their heightened awareness.

"Yes master, I have come to protect your back."

"Come child, we'll walk together a bit. We can talk of things as we return to town center. I only wish to have a few words with the outsiders. They need to know a bit more about who we are, as do the good folks of Fortune's Gateway."

Now, his own curiosity stirring, Bao Ling asked, "Really, what possibly might he want to speak with you about as the two of you returned to town and his anticipated end?"

I Will Let the Story Tell Itself

"Well, we're right back to where we started aren't we? He spoke only of 'the thought cuts,' and as he did, we quickened our pace. I've since come to learn that when Master Li made up his mind to act, he preferred to move forward, straight ahead, rarely to the side, and never rearward in retreat. As we made our way to town center and the grand circle, the townsfolk remained massed. I could see them still listening intently to some finely garbed Wei emissaries sided by their hardened and obviously seasoned knight protectors. The speakers promised generosity and opportunity to all who had the good sense to ally with their soon to be consummated occupation of the province. Master Li turned to me, pointing, 'Up there child, climb to that roof, follow the roof line toward the grand circle, from above you'll be able to see and hear everything. Pay close attention; expect tricks and assassins in the crowd. You will be my eyes from the rear, protect my back by calling to me of any threats or trickery. Whatever happens, be careful and alert. Make sure you take in everything I elect to show them. Consider it my special lesson to you. A gift."

" 'What are you going to show them?' I asked.

"He answered only, 'How my thought cuts!'

" 'But how will I warn you if I see something amiss?'

" 'Stand on the roof, yell "Fire!" and point to the west!' "

Hui paused his recitation at that point. Bao Ling could sense his friend struggling with whether to continue, or just how much more he wished to say or reveal.

Hui looked over to his comrade. Really, if one couldn't keep stock in Bao Ling, well then, who might one trust?

Then, he continued.

"In years subsequent, I've learned of the many particulars from that eventful day, at first from Master Li, then from others. I took great care in mapping them accurately, so that nothing would be lost or overlooked in the retelling. Thinking back, it just seems magical, as if all things were happening as they were supposed to, like a carefully scripted opera. But of course, we knew nothing then. We were in its midst, dropped unexpectedly into a web with stakes too real, and somehow we had to survive. It sure looked grim going in.

"I'd prefer to let you hear the whole story. There's so much more to it than how the thought cuts, or what I alone remember of it from my childhood. Indeed, afterward Master Li engaged it frequently as a training vehicle, for myself and the other novices. He meticulously recounted for us the particulars of what transpired. From his perspective of course, making sure we grasped and understood even the most subtle nuances of why he decided to do things as he did when he did them. 'Nothing happened, but by intent,' he would say. In private, he insisted to me he was wide awake the whole time, while everyone else had dozed off or become muddled in distraction, 'Except for the Fox of course; and you too little one. There would have been no good end, had you fallen prey to distraction. I was most fortunate to have you there, backing me.'

"Actually, he said he was wide awake 'almost' the whole time. You'll understand when we're done. In the beginning, I had no grasp of what he meant by any of this. Being awake? Muddled? Much later, as a monk, aided by rigorous contemplation, my own appreciation of his words eventually came around. And with that, whenever I had reason to revisit the town or travel the lowlands, I made it a point to search for the others who had been involved. I saw the importance of putting it all together, so that I and whoever else heard could see how it made sense, and possessed informing purpose of its own, which is what Li Fung insisted from the first to be the case. 'Seek the guiding thread,' he would tell me.

"Luckily, I found many who were still available, and willing to speak with me. Fortunately, they remembered who I was, even though I had aged, become a monk, and lost an arm. That included the headsman, the adjutant, the games maker, even the supposed thugs, and the pig herder. Despite his injuries, he had defeated the odds and endured, though severely crippled. I even tracked down some who had been among the Wei soldiers, and one of the knights.

They all agreed with me. The events had profoundly affected them all, some even said their lives had taken new courses in the aftermath. The knight, for example, had become caretaker for the pig herder. It just seemed too important to let even the smallest detail slip away unnoticed. To a person, they proved kind and generous in sharing their recollections. The picture I paint for you tonight will be complete, not just in my voice, but in the record of their collective remembrance. I want for you to experience it as if you could be in each of their minds, even hearing their thoughts, able to take it in from every view, every perspective. You'll find the account has a voice of its own, and speaks for itself as to our reality.

"So hold fast and listen carefully, it may take half the night, but I believe you are among those meant to hear it in its entirety."

Fa Miu Stalls Li Fung

Eyes locked and wings tucked like a hawk, Li Fung
angled toward his prey. He pushed briskly through the
milling crowd cutting toward town center where the Wei
delegates and prominent dignitaries gathered for their
speeches, proclamations and presentations. Locals
recognized Li as a great martial arts master, and
deferentially cleared his path. They also knew him to be a
Shu tribesman, though the inflection in his voice hinted he
had once been an aristocrat serving in Chengdu.

They all knew of the goings-on in the hills, and of the
incessant skirmishes between the tribespeople and the Wei
vanguards. It saddened them. On the one hand, they
empathized, even sympathized with the hill people. But, as
proponents of commerce, they also recognized the
opportunities, and knew that timely action on their part
meant quick riches. Though they never openly voiced it,
some among them did indeed feel the hill people had
become an impediment to broadened commerce. Some even
went so far as to conclude the hill people's continued
existence jeopardized their own future. "They have no one

to blame but themselves; the life they've chosen since time immemorial has now become a liability to them, and to everyone else for that matter. Liu Bei[6] is dead. They no longer have a benefactor. We can't do it. Their time, and their usefulness may already have ended. As to their future, well, if the hill people continue to stand in the way of change and prosperity, they too will have to go." Some spoke of relocating them to the western wilderness. There, they wouldn't be in anyone's way, at least not for now.

Those who thought this way would argue nothing guaranteed one's survival so much as the ability to glean wealth from uncertainty and change. There's no better security! Better to be behind the wheel, or riding atop, than beneath it. Why, even Li Fung understood this. In life, everyone moved to their own purpose and end. It was the way of this world, and he could not ignore its timeless momentum. But brazen lies propagated in the very heart of the city? This city, which had in the past befriended, even welcomed, his people? The visitors from Wei predicted the certainty of imminent change throughout the region, doubtless over the carcasses of his tribesmen who remained in a fight for their very existence. A new paradigm is what they forecast. Certain to come they said. The hill people would be defeated they promised, no longer would they delay the future.

---

[6] Liu Bei - One time emperor of the Shu Han, or western empire. He knew that so long as the Shu tribes remained viable, there would be no direct path for Wei to attack from the east. To that end, he ensured the Shu remained independent, and a friendly ally.

This Li Fung could not bear. He would show the truth of the issue, for all to see and consider. Let them witness and measure according to their own judgment. He would set out the truth to stand alongside the lies. Then, trust the folks of Fortune's Gateway to decide rightly their course, their leanings, and their own future.

Fact is, few from Wei had ever fought their way from one end of the Shu range to the other. Those who did never said much of it, or what they had to do to accomplish the feat. For them, it was no less than total immersion into adversity with no seeming end. Assuming one somehow survived, the hardships of the passage could prolong it by many months. There were terrifying rumors of comrades killing comrades over scarce supplies, rampant torture of the natives, even cannibalism when hard necessity dictated. Civilized norms seemed to have no justification or use once the Wei expeditions encountered the many hostile apparitions lurking in the hills and hollows of Shu. Every thought centered on survival, no matter the cost, or what had to be sacrificed. If lucky enough to make it through, one was never the same afterward as when one first entered. Many who survived the ordeal simply continued westward, into their own wilderness, and once there were never seen or heard from again.

Take that as you will!

Sensing the buzz along the rear periphery, the spectators standing frontmost knew immediately something was up. Those in the western plaza parted politely, giving due respect to Li, allowing him clear passage toward the makeshift platform and stage from which his adversaries continued to spit their propaganda and weave their misportrayals.

As he drew near, the prominently seeded enforcers of Wei took quick notice and began to close toward him from all directions. Noting the ominous shifts, supportive elements in the throng coalesced even more tightly around the Wei troopers. The guards, jockeying for position, pushed hard against the pressuring tide; only to be further stymied in their efforts by those still closing from the rear, who, on seeing the need, added their own weight to the crush, clustering the complicit onlookers even more tightly together near the stage. This was not lost on those speaking at the front. Obviously mistaken as to the goings on, they read the forward shifts in those assembled as proof of the power and persuasive elegance of their words over the ever attentive listeners.

Silly isn't it; how easy it is to misread others?

On this day, town adjutant Fa Miu[7] pushed out from the base of the stage and made his way directly into Li's path, putting his right palm forward as though intending to stop Li Fung. He had been sent to do so by the Honorable Liang San, town headsman, who watched apprehensively from the stage. Fa Miu served as his deputy, adviser, sometimes protege and, when necessary, hammer. He had earned this

---

[7] Fa Miu was already known to Bao Ling. This is detailed in another tale where a much older Fa Miu, acting as toll collector, took special interest in Bao Ling and his lady companion Zhi Mei, in the end, gifting them two gold sovereigns, more than offsetting any taxes they had been forced to pay.

trust by his brilliant administration and oversight of town resources, as well as by his systematic collection of taxes supported by detailed accountings of their proper engagement in town development and stimulation of commercial infrastructure. Back then, detailed and proper accounting were rare qualities in the character of a tax collector.

Before Fa Miu, taxes were regulated by the old piece-of-the-action formula. The man at the top got ten percent, as did his enforcer, and then the heads of justice, then of course, the regional authority, as well as the Emperor and his court or in times of flux the warlord equivalent. Don't judge harshly. It insured the peace, kept the ever sniffing noses out of one's immediate affairs, and represented the price of practical freedom from interference. So long as you weren't among the many at the bottom, it usually worked out fine.

With his fox-like cleverness, Fa Miu had found ways around much of that. No one ever knew or suspected anything, so skilled his chicanery. Their concerns weighed upon appearances, not substance. Distinguishing substance from appearance took hard work, which they routinely delegated to others, men like Fa Miu. To his credit, the town books were tight, and perfectly kept. Liang San got his ten percent. The constables were well paid, and Fa Miu insisted their chief be selected on merit and rewarded proportionate to his ability to keep peace and security. Likewise with the justices. As to warlords, and regional authorities, and even Emperors or their equivalents, they too all got their cuts, but the accounts they saw were not the working accounts of record. With numbers, Fa Miu orchestrated magic. Payoffs which in the past had consumed nearly half of all collected revenue (off the top, mind you), were now taking less than a quarter. The money preserved went to development, community sanitation, education for the children, and land purchases for the peasants — basically removing sizable numbers of them from prolonged indenture. So you see, Fa Miu was a very clever fellow; he appreciated the true worth of awareness and made sure to know a great deal about everything, just as he knew how to play his squares[8].

One day, Liang San demanded his take be doubled, a twenty percent cut for himself, rationalizing his being the brains behind the appointment of Fa Miu justified the extra stipend. "No sweat" he reckoned, "Even with my slice off the top, we're still leaving more for the townspeople than they've ever had with any headsman in the past." By his selfish figuring, this still left more than enough for needed development, so, no harm done, right?

People think like that you know! Perhaps even you, standing in his place, might feel the same. Too often is the culprit found to be a product of the circumstance. Temptation is often underappreciated among those who hold our greatest confidence.

Emboldened by anger, Fa Miu responded only that one should learn to be satisfied with what was already a windfall. *"The upstart!"* thought Liang San. *"Doesn't he know he serves at my leisure? If not for me, he'd be selling chickens on the roadside!"* Of course, the now outraged Liang San

---

[8] Fangqi, an ancient board game. Recognizable to many in its modern equivalent, the game of squares.

threatened to discharge Fa Miu and to banish him from the province. "Go live with your peasants if you care for them so much!" is what he said.

Fa Miu, at that time still young and foolish, perhaps even brash, stepped fearlessly right up to Liang San's nose and burst out laughing, countering, "Before you think of sending me off, decide first who will stand here before you and deliver an honest ten percent, while at the same time neutralizing all opposing factions and still somehow managing to grow our city and the surrounds. Show me that person now, and I will leave on my own! Good riddance! Be assured, you will hear my laughter in the distance, as all comes crumbling apart from beneath you. Of course I care for the peasants! Who are we without them? With the lack of appreciation and respect I get around here, I'd just as soon be netting fish with the rice farmers. Don't think for an instant you are the only honey for this bee. Singing evening songs with them would be reward enough for what I bring to their tables. At least out there I'd have one less greedy bastard to deal with!"

Liang San, no stranger to the fighting arts himself, nearly struck at Fa Miu's eyes, so offended was he by the brazen outburst. One single thought checked his impulse. He loved Fortune's Gateway. And he had no doubt Fa Miu felt likewise. Therein lay their grist and connection. Something about the frontier: the wildness, the excitement, never a dull moment. Truly, neither of them ever wanted to be anywhere else. But for that, someone with the talents of a Fa Miu would have hitched his destiny to a more imperial vessel. That thought wasn't lost on Liang San. With either of them gone, what would befall their city, and their people.

Together, they had maneuvered and purchased a very delicate neutrality for the townsfolk. Their efforts to preserve that precarious balance served as catalyst to the years of prosperity which ensued. So, given the practicalities, Liang San checked his rage just as he had so many times before, and no doubt would again when their thoughts crossed purposes. Over the course of this delicate partnership, the outbursts, and angry words between them continued unabated, sometimes broiling over into public view. Odds makers in the taverns would often run lines on who would kill who, and whether Fa Miu would be gone from his post before New Year. But in fact, despite appearances the two became as one. Who would have known? Their rocky and unsettled joining, and constant flare-ups, marked the beginning of a beautiful friendship. The fact no one else seemed to have a clue made the little charade all the more charming and worthwhile. As to reaping personal fortune? Liang San had relaxed his inclination toward superfluous greed. After all, who needed pillage and warlords, when you had the likes of Fa Miu delivering the goods painlessly, and reliably. And on top of that, somehow managing to do great good!

So, as Li Fung quickly approached town center, it fell to Fa Miu, as "grand solver of problems" to deter whatever troubles Li Fung might bring. On this day, he was tasked to be the hammer, should such prove necessary. Though slight and foxlike, in his younger days, Fa Miu was not one to be taken lightly in any encounter.

A Kinship of Sorts

Li stopped from respect for their prior civility, saying only, "Friend Fa Miu, please don't interfere. We have no issues between us. I wish only to visit with, and enlighten our friends from the east."

Fa Miu answered, "I assure it is true Li Fung. We are indeed friends in more ways than you know. Having said that, I must also remind what you are thinking to do today will only bring trouble, where it is neither sought nor desired. On top of that, you'll likely be killed. A tragic waste.

"You understand as well as do I, Li Fung. The emissaries from Wei can not have you humiliate them, and then allow you to walk off. They'll use you to teach us some hard lesson regarding their take on proper decorum and respect. Frankly I've already benefited enough from their harsh teachings and their examples. I have no need or desire to be shown more."

Ever so slightly, pointing with his chin toward the tavern roof at the far plaza's edge, Fa Miu continued, "Besides, what will become of the boy, should you not survive? Worse yet, if he is found to have come with you or to be complicit. Even for the often blind Wei, the child's mountain garb will leave little doubt as to why he is here or who he came with."

Master Li smiled warmly toward Fa Miu, "Fa Miu ... the 'Fox', that's what they say of you. Now I see why. Your eyes dart quickly and see what others miss, and your mind drives to the heart of vulnerability, a rare combination indeed! I too will call you 'Fox' when I see or think of you. Please understand, it will be out of genuine respect and admiration for your gifts.

"The boy is Shi-Hui Ke. I expect he will be fine. Like you, he is clever and resourceful, and knows how to skirt trouble." Li Fung paused for a moment, as though in reflection, then added, "You would do well to remember his name, my friend. Shi-Hui Ke. As for me, perhaps we can share tea after I've spoken to our honored delegates from Wei."

Fa Miu nodded and smiled, "Of course, I should find that to my liking. Be sure to bring your head, lest the tea spill needlessly to the ground."

He remained silent and still from that point, not inclined to move from where he stood. Knowing no more could or needed be said, he yet hoped to preclude tragedy. Using force to stop Li would serve no purpose, except to agitate the crowd, which at this moment was looking for some real excitement to offset the all too predictable babble of the Wei minister, still rattling endlessly on.

Given no other recourse, he could challenge Li himself. He reckoned even odds there. But his heart wasn't in it. It shouldn't surprise you, Fa Miu had ears and eyes that reached far outside Fortune's Gateway. He had hard accounts of the suffering and the torment in the mountains. The Wei felt the riddles of Shu would only be fully unraveled when the Shu people were cleansed from its myriad passages and hideaways. They worked diligently to that end. Still, wherever the Wei went, the damned tribes seemed to infest at every turn. Only those among the tribes who saw the wisdom in turning, and who could be relied upon to unravel the many secrets of the Shu Roads would be tolerated and permitted to remain. But then, who vouchsafed whether they could be trusted, or to what extent? In those times, a question with no seeming end. Who knew whether anyone could be trusted? For his part, Fa Miu felt the Shu were fulfilling a role of great importance and merit. He didn't know why, or how it came to pass, but for generations, they alone shouldered the responsibility of sealing the mountain passages against large scale invasion from the east. Why, even in his humble trading town, legends and songs played regularly as to how the Shu people tricked, foiled, cajoled and unraveled the carefully thought out invasion plans of eastern aggressors. Stories abounded, fables undoubtedly, of how in their most dire moments, they had allied with Monkey King and even today remained under his spells, influence and protection. Who knows why or how such tales emerge. The Shu said little of it. They called the Monkey King by the honorable surname "Sun", and closely guarded what little they knew of his reported doings. Those repelled by the tribes spoke frequently of strange apparitions, and unnatural happenings witnessed and experienced in "those damned hills." Seemingly, everyone wanted control of the cursed roads. It was usually the Wei, but sometimes the Wu, and now, more frequently, remnants or breakaways of the once empires in the form of powerfully ambitious war bands, guided by new generations of would be princes and emperors. All looked to emulate the earlier success of Liu Bei in the far west. How had he made it look so easy? It would make more sense to say one could dance upon the moon than it would to assume one might replicate the deeds of Liu Bei. Whatever drove the Shu tribespeople to their current purpose, there is one thing for which there can be no doubt. It took shape during the reign of Liu Bei, under the counsel and guidance of the peerless Zhuge Liang. From the West, where his kingdom flourished, Liu respected the individuality and unique character of the mountain tribes, even declaring their freedom and full dominion over the Shu Roads. No one had ever done that before. He proclaimed it to be their destiny, and their imperative, which they most proudly accepted.

From hard experience, Liu had learned the 'Rule of Seven'. When defending one's self, one's loved ones, one's domain and one's own freedom; one is seven times more effective than when one moves aggressively upon another elsewhere. So Liu decided "Let them have their mountains, and their ways. We will simply be their friends. Only that course will assure the roads are shut to outsiders." As to particulars, he left them to Minister Zhuge Liang. The Wei would mockingly say, the devil lay in the details. The devil of course being Zhuge Liang, and the details being what he did to empower the Shu people, and at what cost to the Wei.

For the Wei, it's as if he were still there, reading their intent, anticipating their every move. The cursed details, the innumerable tricks and endless networks of devious traps which continually thwarted their efforts.

As to how the Shu tribes met their piece of the bargain, even Liu Bei would come to calculate and applaud their efficacy as; "Far beyond the Rule of Seven." It represented a sacred trust, freely worked out and agreed upon by men greater than could ever be encountered in these new and still troubled times. Besides, until that day where Li Fung found himself standing before Fa Miu, all knew what raged endlessly in the hills had kept Fortune's Gateway secure from eastern invaders. The threats from the West where once Liu Bei's empire thrived, could be managed by the manipulations of Fa Miu. And the enticements of trade, like an unplanned exchange of kind favors, served also to protect the western flanks of the Shu tribes.

So, you see, there was a kinship of sorts, Fortune's Gateway and the Shu Tribes, each providing a genuine blessing to the other.

Why It's a Lie

While he didn't know how it all came to this, nor did he care to, Fa Miu would not ever desecrate such a profound understanding rooted in complete trust.

With that thought, he stepped aside for Li to pass. The crowd ahead parted even more, clearing a wide channel for Li's final approach to the stage. Some among flashed smiles of encouragement, anticipating the eruption likely to follow.

Just before he stepped free from the crowd, and was finally met by Wei's security, Li glanced back to Fa Miu.

For a fleeting moment their eyes locked. No words passed from lips, but Fa Miu heard the request, *"Will you see to the boy should I fall?"*

He seemed for all purposes to have turned away in anger and frustration at Li Fung. A pretext of course, made to ensure his own head remained in its place. No one had reason to notice or suspect the subtle nod of acknowledgment which, hidden in the turning, sealed his promise to Li Fung.

From the stage, Headsman Liang San glared at Fa Miu. His aide would pay for this failure, and the resulting embarrassment. *"This time,"* he thought, *"We're through. Finished! I really mean it, dammit!"*

Now assured the boy would be looked after, Master Li pivoted again toward the podium just as the two nearest guards lowered their spear points to bar his entry. To their surprise, his pace accelerated, it seemed he intended to impale himself, walking unflinchingly toward the rightmost spear tip. Without breaking stride, he timed the movement of his hands to his right foot as it stepped forward with authority, angling slightly right of the man to his front. Both his arms raised and floated lightly and non-threateningly, settling into the classic right hand forward, "playing the lute". It could have been a dance step.

The Wei guards of course did not know how to take this, even less, how to react. When on strange turf, you don't kill the natives simply for lifting their arms. The befuddled guard attempted to reposition his spear, centering its point on Li's sternum.

By then, it was too late. Engaging the subtle angle of his arms against the spear, Master Li's left hand snake coiled the shaft from above, then gripped its bottom. The movement delicately shifted the guard's balance, which Li's right hand further offset with a barely perceptible palm press further up the beam. Then he lu'd[9] ... a classic move where in this instance, he angled the spear tip downward, grounding it to his left. To avoid falling flat on his face, the guard skillfully dropped his stance, sat low, and pulled the staff horizontally back in, expecting to recover.

Li Fung of course foresaw this reaction, even allowed for it, and as the guard pulled, Li added his own weight to what now transformed into a forward push on the shaft, no different than ringing a temple bell. Then he tightly gripped the pole and looped both hands leftward.

The subtle, but dramatic shift in tension, gave the guard nowhere to go but directly into his partner, now staring in disbelief at what unfolded alongside. Why, some in the crowd say they saw the helpless guard lifted completely from the ground by Li's sorcery.

Simple basics, that's all it was. But in the hands of a master, true magic. Both guards, now without their feet or their roots, spilled clumsily over. Li vociferously apologized, and to make a good show of it, labored dutifully to help each return to his feet. Then he mock dusted them

---

[9] Lu, one of the eight essential energies underlying the internal arts. They are:

Peng - to ward off
Lu - to roll back or empty
Ji - to press
An - to push
Cai - to pluck or grasp
Lie - to split
Zhou - elbow strike
Kao - shoulder strike

off, and handed back their weapons, offering, "My regrets. Your sharpened points seemed for a moment to be directed my way. As you can see, I bear no weapons. I mean no harm, and pose no threat[10]."

The crowd laughed at the display.

Before either could answer or detain him further, he jumped full shoulder height onto the stage, like a panther about to engage his prey. There, the seasoned knight guardians attending Wei Lord Minister Long Hsieh were clearly not amused, nor intending to be so easily duped. Li Fung counted five of them.

Headsman Liang San wanted no bloodbaths defiling his town center, either on stage, or between the Wei regulars and the crowd, among whom they had been carefully seeded beforehand. Yes, he cared for the mountain people, and he even cared for Li Fung, but not over the long term interests of Fortune's Gateway. As the first knight drew his blade and advanced on Li, a roar emitted from the audience, making their displeasure dead certain. Headsman Liang San stepped quickly between; just as Long Hsieh issued at the

---

[10] An adaptation of an adage variations of which exist in many schools and systems of martial arts:

I come to you with only my empty hands
I bear no weapons.
Should I be forced to defend myself, my principles, or my honor;
Should it be a matter of life or death, or right or wrong;
Then here are my weapons.
My empty hands.

last instant, his belayed signal for the knight to stand down. The remaining four positioned to the ready, and on Long Hsieh's approving nod, all spread into a five pointed star skirmish pattern. To a bird viewing from above, the western front edge of the stage formed the star's base. Li Fung stood surrounded in the center, facing directly east. Three knights stood to his front, and two were behind him, their geometry forming the points of the star. This assured all combat angles were tight and under their control.

Li scrutinized the surrounding warriors closely. By their garb and its distinct colorations, he concluded they were a fraternity of skilled and well honed professionals. Assassins, if you will. Starting with the one on his left, and circling rightward, he saw their extravagant tunics colored black, green, red, yellow and white. Each bore meticulous ornamentations highlighting the animal forms taken as their individual totems, all according to established symbolic precedents. For royal knights, nothing could be left to chance. Their roles and respective inclinations aligned by design and tactical intent with the characteristics of the five elements and their cryptic underlying metaphysics[11]. All of it undoubtedly rooted in the Classic of the Changes, which Li Fung knew as well as anyone. Black (full yin), the color of heaven, would belong to the leader, and as expected, he took the northern point. He would be their guiding star. Green, the ascending dragon, represented new yang, or yang

---

[11] Black - heavenly tortoise; full yin; North
Green-Azure Dragon; New Yang; East
Red - Vermillion Bird; full yang; South
Yellow - Yellow Dragon; balance; Center
White - White Tiger; New Yin; West

blossoming, and like the sunrise, anchored east directly to Li's front. Red, or fire, the embodiment of yang, would hold south, off to Li's right. Yellow was a most interesting chap. He balanced and harmonized the energy of the group, being neither yin, nor yang. As pivot and catalyst for the others, he always inclined by nature toward their center, where on this day, the tribesman Li already stood. Yellow, personifying the yellow dragon within whom all energies found their equilibrium, looked menacingly at Li, as though the unwanted intruder had usurped the core, precisely where Yellow expected to stake his end claim. For now, he would secure position behind Li's right shoulder. Alongside, and further to the left stood White, far enough back so as to pose no immediate threat. That was his way, the seemingly recessive, but ruthlessly lethal white tiger. His color, white represented new yin, or yang departed.

Li Fung angled his head one way, then the other. Satisfied he had fixed their locations, he mused, *"The Yellow Knight glares at me as though I were holding his child. I can feel the rising tide of his anger. He wants center and I stand where he looks. He frowns his displeasure my way."*

Li could sense how in spirit, Yellow harbored the essence or soul of the group and embodied the needed ballast which assured their ability to react effectively to every situation and condition. Li smiled knowingly, thinking to himself, 'Yellow, long recognized to be the color of warriors and heroes.'

"Master Li," called Liang San, "I was not told you would be coming today, or that you planned to interrupt our esteemed guests in their presentation of thoughts, options and opportunities for developing better relations and contacts with their kingdom to the east."

"Begging your patience and your understanding Honorable Liang San, we knew nothing of this event prior to making our usual rounds in trade and commerce. We learned of the guests from Wei only while we attended to our business affairs. After seeing their presence and their purpose, and out of respect for the goodwill of the townsfolk which we have always enjoyed, we elected to leave with dispatch, though still puzzling how our mortal enemies were now inexplicably welcomed here, and could be seen milling about Fortune's Gateway as though it had become their home."

First murmurs, then a rumble came from the crowd, making clear their displeasure and their concern for the dignity and integrity of the mountain folk.

"I too might have left without issue, but as I passed through town center, I could not help but to overhear Minister Long Hsieh forecasting our ultimate end before winter."

"What of it? As our official guest, is he not welcome and free to speak his mind?" replied Headsman Liang San.

"Why it's a lie, or if not a lie; an intolerable fabrication which should not be allowed to be voiced or repeated. Certainly not here of all places, where a man's honesty, and his integrity have always secured his bond. Perhaps it is not the same in the east. If so, it falls to us to show the proper way." He cast a glance at the enraged Wei emissaries.

Li Fung
"I could not help but to overhear..."

Master Li Engages the Wei

The stalled knights moved forward to tighten the perimeter encircling Master Li. Minister Long Hsieh now verged on ordering his execution. Seeing this Liang San quickly interrupted, "Explain yourself Li Fung. We all know the struggles of your people; and also, why they have come upon you. We can not save your people from destiny, or fate, or even natural change. But we are not your enemies."

"There is more in our resistance than you know Liang San. We fight for what is ours, and our freedom, and our birthright to enjoy and engage with it. We ask nothing more. When the dogs who have predicted our end have finished their feast, where do you suppose they will look next? Are there not other feasts to be had?"

Silence … everywhere … as though all awaited Liang San's reply. The meaning had not been lost on anyone.

He, of course, could say nothing. He knew what Li Fung meant, just as he knew a dead town head was as good as no town head at all.

Shi-Hui Ke listened intently from the roof top.
Witnessing the events unfolding below, he whispered to
himself, "Aaaahhhh, if this be what he meant, the thought
does indeed cut."

Li Fung took advantage of the continuing silence, the
crowd still motionless, and attentive.

He continued, "They will not conquer us by winter!
That's been said many times before, and has never borne
out. True, they torment and abuse our people, poison our
waters, seed us with disease, enslave our women, tempt and
steal our young men. But our Shu Mountains have a mind
of their own. As do we, the mountains disdain the very
thought of them, and sicken from their feet touching upon
its surface. These Wei offer nothing new. Frankly, I find
their predictability stupefying. Like all invaders before
them, they incessantly over reach and look to propagate
their poisoned wills and unbridled exploitations on all who
resist or impede their boundless greed and ambition."

"And how do you suppose the Shu people will avoid
what has already been ordained by heaven?" asked the
minister, wearing a mock face of interested curiosity. He
spoke and looked as though heaven were indeed behind
him. Perhaps next he would argue how all their lives would
be improved under Wei's civilizing hand.

For an instant, Long Hsieh's confidence unedged Li
Fung. *"Might it be possible they had the celestials on their side?*

"What if I reached with my hand this very moment through Long Hsieh's naval and ripped his heart out for all to see. Would that too be because heaven ordained it? Or because I chose to do it? Would his heart be dark and gangrened, or red like my own? What I understand of heaven is if heaven stood anywhere, it seemed to be in the midst of all our uncertainty, and the chaos ever surrounding. I've found it nowhere else. What lessons has the minister overlooked from these past four hundred years? How could he have missed the unequivocal declaration of heaven's true intent — push mankind to the brink? I'm a practical man, who places his people first. That's all there is to it. It matters not where the celestials stand on these issues, I will do what I must, heaven be damned!"

"Look to heaven if you will Long Hsieh, we have no issue with it, or anyone else for that matter, until they defile our land and seek to exterminate us. Should that be heaven, so be it. We will be the other.

"This I know with certainty, neither you, nor anyone in the Wei court truly speaks for destiny. Be assured, I speak for the mountain people. We make our own, and pay for it with our blood and our spirits. I tell you now, in front of all these witnesses; we, the Shu people will protect our domain, and no one will replace us. We and the land are one. As to the mountains, and the roads, we the Shu people are their voice, and their will. There stands our heaven! Ask your armies wandering the endless mazes what they think has been ordained by heaven when their food and supplies run out, and the once nourishing waters surrounding them dry to parched sand."

Long Hsieh already had his words ready, "Say and think what you will. Yes, we are offended by your insolence, but we too are guests here, and will respect the propriety of our hosts. As to the future, your future? We all know, and that includes every person standing here today, the Shu people are finished."

"Hardly finished. I can speak on this with confidence, having seen with my own eyes. The Wei will not be here by winter. The victories they proclaim in the mountains are fictions at best, fabrications and lies at worst. History and legend record how the ministers of the once supreme Cao Cao came here with the same message, in this very square. Where are they now? Look, yet standing before you today are the Shu, in full possession of their integrity and their domain. And because of their sacrifice over generations, the people of Fortune's Gateway have prospered against all odds and adversaries."

The crowd remained silent, as seeded Wei guards glared about scouting for prey. Any overt sign of support would be met with detention, and who knew what else?

"Kill him!" ordered Long Hsieh who turned summarily away, but not before Liang San stepped forward and boldly ordered, "There will be no bloodshed here today! Wei may be great on the other side of the world, but here, we are the authority. You and your representatives are guests in our home, as are the tribes-people of Shu." A roar of support emitted from the crowd, leaving a surprised Long Hsieh no doubt as to the thinness of his footing. This diversion served to cloak Headsman Liang San's signal for the town constables to close along the edge of the platform. What little law there was in the frontier was provided by these same town constables. Though remote, a commercial center like Fortune's Gateway had much to lose if not properly protected. Their constables were respected and feared, even though they might not be the equal of Wei's knights, now on display in their full regalia. Fortunately, they made up with numbers what they may have lacked in battle guile. Long Hsieh had no choice but to rein his muscle in.

Mayor Liang pondered for a moment on what he might do next.

One thing for sure. Tomorrow, if he lived, he would drink wine with Fa Miu, whom he had now completely forgiven.

A Circular Challenge

While Mayor Liang pondered, Fa Miu studied and Long Hsieh fumed. It fell to Li Fung to do the thinking for everyone and somehow break this icy stalemate.

Finally, he spoke, "We seek no bloodshed here. The visitors from Wei are guests under the protection of headsman Liang, as am I. I'm sure I stand with Minister Long Hsieh on this point. We will respect propriety and not cause our honorable host to lose face on our account."

Long Hsieh grunted begrudgingly, adding, "Then you agree to leave, and allow us to continue without further interruptions?"

A long, almost interminable pause followed as Liang San, Long Hsieh, Fa Miu and the warriors of Wei scrutinized Li Fung in anticipation of his reply.

"I must beg your kind indulgence on this. I agree to leave, but only after I have had opportunity to provide my brief but unimpeachable demonstration of Shu's position on their future, contrary to that portrayed by the good emissaries."

Long Hsieh barked, "You will leave when Liang San orders you to leave!" He stared hard at Liang San as he said this, clearly expecting an order for Li to vacate the stage.

Liang San raised his left hand motioning Long Hsieh to hold his tongue, "Honorable Minister, please allow, I will speak for myself on this matter. We owe much to the Shu people and their sacrifices, and we do not take our debt lightly. While today we extend our hospitality and reciprocal friendship to the guests from Wei, we do not forget our troubled history, now hopefully locked in the vaults of time and forever behind us. The same can not be said for the good people of Shu, who, by your own words, should be eliminated by winter. I can not resist but to question whether you said the very same of us in the halls of Wei."

For once, Fa Miu smiled appreciatively, surprised by his usually timid principal's new found audacity.

Turning to Li Fung, Liang San continued, "And what is it you have in mind to do, Li Fung?"

Li Fung smiled, "A simple contest, nothing more."

Long Hsieh, brushed close to Liang San and allowed, "We will defer to you on this. Our only wish remains for Fortune's Gateway to prosper as our sister city, and for harmonious relations between us." Then he whispered only for the ears of Liang San, "Be very careful with this man. For you and your people, he spells trouble."

Liang San politely smiled as though to acknowledge the seeming accommodation, then continued, "Well said Honorable Minister. Friend Li Fung, tell us about your contest."

Li Fung went to the town scribe, who had been recording events of the day, borrowed some ink and a horse tail brush, then set about to mark a circle, bounded within the five points of the tactical star assumed by Long Hsieh's body guards. They had to step back as Li Fung brushed by them, begging their indulgence.

Such games of the mind sometimes play important when setting the field for contest.

In the middle of the circle, he drew the character for Shu, then for benefit of the crowd, walked about the circle while the Knights of Wei returned to their five points, standing just outside the conspicuous line and it's still drying ink.

Once the townspeople understood the geometry of the ring, Master Li stepped before Liang San, "A simple game, based upon a supposition." Now he made sure his voice carried and projected from the stage to the ever more curious crowd pressing about. From the corner of his eye, he spied the boy Shi-Hui Ke stationed at his rooftop vantage point, peering cautiously over the top of a ridge beam, head resting upon bi-pod arms visible only to one who already knew to look for him there.

Master Li proceeded to define his challenge. "Within the circle, we have everything Shu. Outside the circle, we have the worlds of others. Perhaps they exist elsewhere in circles of their own, or perhaps they hover seemingly everywhere, like the wind." He glanced to the Minister as he said this, his meaning clear. "As you can see (he gestured to all those packed about in town center), the good townspeople have no vested interest, or anything to gain or lose from what happens within this circle. That's what I hear, anyway. Some might disagree. But here, (he turns and gestures to each of the stationed knights, then stares across to Long Hsieh), by their demeanor and their words, it is clear something within the circle draws their complete interest. Who knows what?"

Laughingly he adds, "I don't think any of them would trade their lives for mine. Yet they seek to purge us from our homes, the homes of our ancestors, and the resting places of our forbears. Do we threaten them? Anyone? Are we so hostile and uncivilized as to be deemed a troublesome pest? Good townspeople, you know the answers to these questions, as do I. It is for that reason, I declare to all of you now. I claim the circle! Inside rests the heart of my people (pointing to the character 'Shu' as he says this), an insignificant detail to others perhaps, but to me, to us, everything. Our home, our ways, our natures, our beliefs, our freedom. No one can take this from us; not before winter; not ever. Today, I will prove my point.

"For our game, I propose we let the townspeople see for themselves how well the Shu tend to what they deem to be theirs, particularly when their will and determination are pit against the designs of powerful others (again drawing their attention to the five knights and the Minister Long Hsieh)."

One of the knights bursts in, "Someone, bring him weapons."

Headsman Liang San interrupted, "No weapons, no wanton bloodshed, this must be better played!"

Li Fung answered, "Of course, that is my intention. A simple game to ease the gravity of the moment, and to entertain the crowd. I will stand here, centered atop the character for 'Shu'. The knights from Wei will each in turn attempt to take the circle from me. If they remove me from within, I will concede the circle to them, and they will have their victory. Should they fail, my point will be made."

A skeptical Long Hsieh asked, "That's it?"

"Not entirely. Respecting our commitment not to intrude excessively into your plans for this day, I will agree to limit the window of the contest, with Honorable Liang San keeping the time, and declaring the winner once time has run. A sandglass perhaps, or the span of a burning incense stick?"

Already anticipating this, a resourceful merchant in the throng had sandglass at the ready, which he placed atop a table at stage's edge where all could see it clearly, sand ready for the running. Liang San picked it up and studied it, if only to satisfy himself enough time would be allotted for a true and credible contest. Once satisfied, he set it down and side glanced to Long Hsieh. Hearing no objections, he turned fully to the Minister and said, "Granted, a harmless game, yet, an imposition on your time, and your program for this day. It is within your rights to reject Li Fung's proposal, and ask he simply leave, with no further interruption."

As proposed, Long Hsieh could see no advantage to the game. He remained sure his trusted knights would win with ease. Why, they were twice Li's size, obviously better proportioned, and undoubtedly better tested in actual combat. Even with their assured victory, it proved nothing to anyone to defeat someone who looked like he couldn't win in the first place. *"So ... why even play? Where can there be advantage in this?"*

Finding no answer, but not wanting to summarily reject a scenario where his points might be even more firmly driven home, he turned with whetted curiosity to Li Fung, "Honorable Li, setting our differences aside for a moment. If you will be so kind as to help me understand. For what reason would I agree to have my knights participate in your escapade, if in defeating you, nothing is gained that we don't already have?"

"Why, we're fighting for Shu of course, and access to the mountain passages," answered Li Fung.

Gasps, and then, silence. The crowd emitted a rumble from its core, each seemingly asking the other what they thought they had just heard.

Stunned by the response, Long Hsieh said, "No games sir! We're fighting for a circle on a wooden platform. I ask again, can you give me a reason why we should humor your challenge?"

Master Li looked for support to Liang San, who said in turn, "Minister, I believe Li Fung has wagered the Shu Roads in his challenge."

"Ridiculous, every person here knows he has no authority to do that!"

"To the contrary Minister Long. A Supreme Council of five governs the coalition of hill tribes. Because of their history, and the demands set upon them, it has long been the practice that each of the five speaks with full authority for the group. By their respective deeds have they earned their people's highest trust. Here, in Fortune's Gateway, this has been forever understood, and respected, as it underpins the foundation for a long tradition of transactions, credit, and delivery on promises made."

"... and Li Fung is one of them? One of the five known to have authority to bind the group?"

"Yes" assured Liang San, "This I know with certainty. His word seals all transactions, and has never faltered. Unless he deems fit to correct my humble misunderstanding of his proposal, to be clear, Honorable Li Fung has staked the Shu Roads and his people's withdrawal from resistance, against your acceptance of his challenge."

Shocked by this seemingly cavalier abandonment of his people's best interests, the headsman looked to Master Li

69

Fung, clearly showing his displeasure over the reckless wager. "I ask only for Li Fung to confirm this."

"Yes … as you said. Confirmed!"

Long Hsieh turned to Li Fung and asked, " … and what do we forfeit should we lose to you."

"I will demonstrate by deed who my people are and why the Shu mountains and ranges will forever remain our home. The price for my victory will be the simple abandonment of your lies and misportrayals. After today, when you speak of us, you will recall what you have seen, and not what you have been told to say."

Liang San reached for Long Hsieh's arm as he stepped gamely forward in fury toward Li Fung; almost forcibly steering him away from Li and toward the crowd.

"Good people of Fortune's Gateway, will you stand as final witness to Master Li's challenge as proposed, and the consideration tendered?"

The crowd roared its unanimous affirmation, then waited expectantly.

"Minister Long Hsieh, do you accept the challenge and terms as stated?"

"I have told no lies, misportrayed nothing!"

Someone from the crowd called for all to hear, "Accept the terms. They are fairly put. Let the play of the game determine what will be said, or done, in the future."

Hearing this, Long Hsieh thought for a moment how his future might look if he returned to court with Shu's submission in hand. The prospect of unbounded reward against his promise to forgo a few harmless fibs should the contest, against all probabilities, be lost on this day. Hardly a gamble, all things considered.

He turned to Li Fung and gave the locked forefinger sign signaling acceptance, which Li Fung accepted by reciprocating the gesture.

Liang San turned to the scribe, instructing, "Let it be so recorded."

The young child still witnessing could only think, *"This thought cuts far too deeply. Master Li Fung, what have you done to us?"*

"Master Li Fung, what have you done to us?"

A Promise Is a Promise

All agreed. Honorable Liang San would stand as judge and referee. The scribe would keep time with the sandglass. Once Liang San signaled action to commence, the glass would be turned. The match would be concluded when Li Fung was thrown or pushed from the circle, or the sand ran out, whichever came first.

Sandglasses were not common in those days. The remarkable instrument came in with the trade from the silk roads, and local artisans were yet attempting to master the art of glass making, looking to perfect the necessary precision. Some even felt water to be a superior medium, since it could be easily replenished and time could run continuously. This particular glass would have been useful to govern the time allotted to a negotiation, or mediation, which was its likely use within this business driven community. In fact, Liang San did indeed turn it when he first set it down, and noted how its run more than matched the span of their active negotiations on stage. He judged from what remained, in total enough for three casual cups of tea. Certainly ample time for a fairly played contest.

Liang San called for Li Fung to take his position within the ring. Master Li stepped center into the circle, weight evenly distributed over the character 'Shu', facing toward the crowd. Many voiced their encouragement to him, knowing the unfortunate odds, and not expecting him to stand a chance. Bets were offered by games makers already hawking methodically among the throng. As headsman, Liang San made sure to allow ample time for the sporting action to build. At first, given the slim prospects, few among the crowd would risk their hard earned silver or gold on Li. They saw no choice but to play the safe, sure bet. Because of that, the line on Li soon escalated. Hoping to pull more easy money into the game, the gamesters gave unprecedented odds to entice those stuck on the fence.

Liang San instructed the match would commence the instant he issued the order to begin, whereupon he would turn the sandglass and set it on the table to be monitored independently by the scribe. All concurred.

Fa Miu, if only to encourage the unlikely, found a gamesman in the crowd and placed his own sovereign on Li Fung. He expected nothing but hoped for a miracle. He would have placed some for Liang San too, but for the appearance of impropriety.

Liang San ordered the scribe to track the time and to call warnings at half way, three quarters, and end approaching, also being sure to call 'ting xialai!' (stop) when the sand had finally run. Once stopped, Liang San would formally declare the winner. All were ready, the five Knights of Wei had met and banked their strategy, Li Fung stood motionless.

"So much at stake, Master Li. What have you gotten us into?," whispered the boy from his post on the roof. For a moment, even he felt compelled to do or come up with something, anything to offset the weight of catastrophe sure to follow. He scoured below, hoping for what he could exploit to advantage, but found nothing. He felt carefully for the goatskin pouch, now hanging cross shoulder. Before entering town square, Master Li Fung had entrusted his purse to the lad, charging, "Should anything happen, take this back to the hills and deliver it to the elders. Unable to harness his curiosity, Shi-Hui Ke had already checked its contents and found there were five gold sovereigns inside. In those times, a life's savings. *"One for each Wei Knight"*, thought the child.

Funny how children think. He reckoned Li to be all but finished. Though formidable in many ways, Master Li now stood overmatched. Even in the remote hills, legends of Wei's Knights and their astounding accomplishments echoed frequently among the evening's fireside go rounds of tales. No one relished the reality of the knight heroes being among their mortal enemies from Wei, but credit was given where credit due. Their amazing deeds could not be denied or ignored; nor could their noble code and high standards ... all like sugar for young imaginations.

Shi-Hui Ke had not reached the age of sophistication and experience wherein he could understand what motivated such tales, and how even the grossest of pigs might be polished into subjects of admiration by those possessing the requisite skills. He did know, however, he had been dealt a conundrum. If the tales proved true, and the professed powers real, he, though a child, would be a goner too. He could not escape unnoticed, and if caught, would be linked immediately to Li. What would become of him and the sovereigns then?

So, now he did the only thing which made sense to his all too clear child's logic.

He snuck down from his rooftop perch just long enough to find one of the gamesmen taking bets in the square. Seeing Fa Miu making his own wager, he studied the bet taker's face and demeanor carefully, then decided it to be a kind face and a fellow he knew could be trusted. Fa Miu certainly seemed comfortable with him.

Once Fa Miu departed, the child went quickly to the gamesman where he put the entire purse up for wager. Taking in the child's mountain garb, the bookmaker hesitated, then questioned, "Where are your friends?" He wasn't overly suspicious, so much as curious. The boy was alone after all. With the purse now counted and in hand, the gamesman could simply pocket it, no one would know the difference. Perhaps the thought crossed his mind. The child said nothing. He meant no disrespect, he could not answer what he did not know, and he could not lie. Even a child could read the temptation shadowing the games maker's eyes.

Now confident the boy was alone, the gamesman queried, "A small fortune lad, where did you get it?" Shi-Hui Ke raised his head pointing chin toward the figure of

Master Li, standing solitary on stage. Not quite a lie, but close enough to make the boy's face flush red with guilt.

"Damn!" thought the handicapper, *"That changes things."*

"This is on Li Fung?"

Feeling older than his age, perhaps charmed by the mystique of courting chance, the boy nodded an authoritative "Yes."

No more needed to be said, the gamesman could see what was what. He stared hard at the boy, "Remember my face boy, if Li Fung wins, you must come find me. I will make an honest accounting to you."

The child did not ask for, and received no receipt or proof of his wager.

One wonders what would make a child do something like this, so seemingly irresponsible.

Then the boy spoke, "Sir, we place this wager for the people of Shu. Should something pass where Master Li or I am unable to claim winnings, I trust you will hold it for the elders of Shu when they come to take us home."

The man nodded his head solemnly, thinking, *"How can it be such a fine child must bear the weight of such concerns?"*

The boy noticed some adjoining people staring, now pointing toward him, a very bad sign. Before the gamesman could reply further, Shi-Hui Ke had vanished.

The boy had his own thoughts on all of this. He figured if Li Fung lost, he would leave the stage in disgrace, and walk alone into the western emptiness, never to be heard from again. Doubtless, soldiers from Wei would be sent to ensure that prospect. Before going, not privy to its loss in wager, Li would instruct young Hui to hold the purse, and return it to the mountains. They would split up to ensure the boy's chance of escape. Perhaps an exercise in futility, since neither would expect the child to make it on his own, given what would already have transpired. Mere sport for the pursuers. Still, he would give it his all, as Master Li had always taught him to do. As to his folly, Hui figured no one would ever know or find out. He would simply say nothing about it. As he saw it, the only consequences to him would come if Li somehow won. Though unlikely, Hui liked the thought of such a dilemma, as it had its roots in success against the fabled warrior saints of Wei. How small would seem his wrongdoing when set against the weight of such a remarkable achievement.

So, though a child's logic, it made perfect sense (to him). Young Hui would stake everything on Master Li winning the challenge. Even with that, there were great risks, but he determined the best plan would be to trust Master Li, hope for the best, and in the end leave town with his teacher, better off than when they came. He would take the heat for risking everything on the uncertain match, perhaps even daring to point out his teacher had risked far more in staking the challenge with Shu. He merely followed the example already set. Who could fault him for that? He smiled at his own cleverness.

As the boy made haste to return to his hideaway, his unexpected motion in the stillness of the crowd also drew the studied attention of Long Hsieh.

Long Hsieh, curiosity aroused over the presence of a solitary child of Shu, followed his hurried exit, then saw him disappear into an alley, re-emerge over a porch, shimmy up a beam, then vault onto a roof.

"Damn people move like monkeys," he thought.

Though pretending not to notice, he saw where the boy scoured about the rooftops for perch. Looking to leave no advantage unplayed, he motioned for the captain of his guard and ordered a squad be dispatched discretely to apprehend the child.

Though Fa Miu had not seen the child in the crowd, the lingering gaze of Long Hsieh on the audience and the focused trace of his stare on something he closely studied caught Fa Miu's interest. He knew from experience, on days like this nothing happened without reason. Seeing no overt explanation for Long Hsieh's behavior triggered his concern. What validated it came moments afterward when the captain of Long Hsieh's guard hurried from the stage and ordered a squad of five toward the west perimeter, pointing them generally to where Fa Miu already knew a young mountain child stood vulnerable to unimagined perils if caught.

He decided it best to investigate personally. A promise after all was a promise.

On stage, it was time. All eyes now turned to Liang San,
who lifted the sandglass for his final inspection, ensuring
bottom half full; top half empty. He readied to turn it over
onto the table, and to declare the commencement of action.

He checked first to see all stood primed for what
promised to follow. All affirmed, by look, nod, glance, or
twitch of nose. Master Li Fung smiled politely and blinked
his ever friendly eyes. He turned to the North, centering
himself on the Black Knight, a gesture of respect, then set.
He stood as he would normally, relaxed, rooted, hands at his
sides, right foot a hair's breadth ahead of the left, the
"ready" stance drummed into his head from nearly the day
of his birth on some remote Shu hilltop.

Five Gold Sovereigns

Warming up the Audience

Careful to avoid telegraphing any sign, the Green Knight readied his mind to charge ruthlessly from the east, looking to lock onto Li Fung's much smaller frame. He and his 'brothers' had planned this. Of the group, the Green Knight was their best at Jiao Li (traditional grappling). While not the strongest fighting style when facing multiple attackers; it reigned virtually supreme one on one, particularly with such a mismatch in size and body mass as this.

Not that Li Fung stood short of stature. On the surface he appeared thin, looking even hungry at times. Back home, concerned matrons would typically want to sit him down for a good meal. With his ever relaxed posture, he gave the impression of being leaner and shorter than he was in fact. He liked to think of himself as very compressed, and when necessity dictated, able to expand at will. It had proven to be a great talent, that no enemy had ever been quite able to decipher. No sooner might you grab at his wrist than your grip had already begun to stretch open. You would think forces from within the wrist pushed irresistibly outward in all directions.

Spooky stuff!

And that's just scratching the surface!

On closer inspection, one reckoned his height to be slightly over eight chi[12]; his physique clean and lean. Due to scarcity, the mountain people habitually ate to sate their gnawing appetites, knowing in those hard times little remained beyond that. Their ethos would not allow for their forgetting the elderly, the infirm, the weak, the wounded and the recovering. All of them, even those otherwise impaired, filled needed social roles, and contributed as their capacities allowed to the well being of the community. The community deemed all to be equal, and acted accordingly. In that way, more than any other, they felt themselves integrally different from the outsiders.

Though not physically imposing as a people, what they lacked in bulk, they compensated for in sturdiness of ligament and impeccable balance. Like fine instruments, their bodies were attuned to the rigorous dictates of their harsh environment, a place where weakness gained no respite. Accustomed to the thin air at altitude, they moved like thoroughbreds in the enriched lowland atmosphere. Seemingly never tiring, they proved capable of prodigious

[12] During the time period in question, a "chi" would have been considered to be the distance between the outstretched tips of one's forefinger and thumb, a casual measurement which might vary from 8 to 9.5 inches. Today, the measurement is set at 1/3 meters (1.094 feet). Li would have stood approximately 5'8" tall, taller than most, but barely reaching the shoulders of even the shortest Wei knight.

exertions if called upon by necessity or the demands of contact with the flatlanders. Of course, in their own domain their stamina proved to be of greater advantage. Most who pursued them into the high country found themselves reduced and exhausted from inability to draw adequate oxygen from the thinned air. If they remained at altitude too long, many became unstable, diminished and confused. Others became incapacitated with unending fits of vomiting, or cranium splitting headaches. Some fell, or jumped, to their deaths. Their leaders provided quantities of the usual herbs to counter this. A pointless exercise, since most found them of little benefit in overcoming the misery.

As lowlanders, Knights typically ate to build their size, and their strength, leaving nothing to chance, fate, or nature. Seeing one of them alongside a townsperson made clear the distinction. To all appearances, they might have been a different type of being, perhaps more reminiscent of Colonel Sun's[13] kind, but that is only a thought. Their arms bulged like melons supported by frames that rippled tightly beneath their tunics, all mounted on tree trunks that on others would have been mere legs. Seeing them, one wondered where nature stopped and sinister wizardry stepped in. Rumors flowed of mysterious edibles brought in from distant places which worked wondrous changes over their bodies. Some were no longer recognizable even to their own parents. When not in actual combat, they continued to practice

---

[13] Colonel Sun. Honored officer and counselor in the service of Liu Bei. Close comrade to Zhuge Liang, and colleague to Guan Yu. Possibly an immortal, possibly a descendant of a different species forever shrouded in mystery, except for his size, demeanor, and awe inspiring presence. We speak of him at length elsewhere, in other stories.

diligently, knowing favors of chance and serendipity could never be counted upon. How well they epitomized the maxim, "You are how you train. A skill will not submit to your command without thousands of repetitions already in your account." They had earned their enviable lifestyles through hard work and sacrifice. Though in their world, all became available to their beckon, complacency remained out of the question. Many aspirants approached from below or behind, ever coveting the same for themselves, looking someday to knock one or the other from his perch and to fill the vacant spot. Knights were sworn to accept all challenges, and did. But not without first reserving the privilege accruing to those already knighted, of resorting to anything to eradicate any threat to their status quo. Understandably, they saw Li Fung as one in a procession of many, in this instance, a most inconvenient ripple. In another light, perhaps a chance for some carefree play. An opportunity to hone their craft.

On this, Li Fung had their advantage. He knew them, and had seen them, or if not them, the likes of their cloned brothers in the eastern ranges. He had been careful to scrutinize and study their movements and tactics while in the field of battle; just as he had seen and, at first, been horrified by their sense of 'play'. In time, he hardened, numbed and adjusted to what he had witnessed. It served to steel his determination. Though not inclined to return atrocities, he kept within himself a ledger, always remembering what he had beheld, and who had done it. He believed in karma and trusted justice would eventually show its head in the accounting. He looked someday to be the hand wielding its hammer strike of retribution, and prepared himself accordingly. He too knew, "You were how you trained."

Going in, the knights joked openly and not too discreetly about Li Fung's carcass soon to be sailing helplessly from the stage. A clear message from Wei, no quarter would be given to rebels, or those otherwise resisting or opposing. The sooner the point delivered, the sooner the entourage could leave this forsaken outpost. Simply put, being in their way meant death! One of them even bought a pig from a village simpleton, dressed it up and introduced it to the crowd as the great "Master Li Fung" moderating the action while another summarily strangled the life from it. Then for a bit of warmup and added display, they tossed it among themselves around the ring, trashing one another over who had hurled it furthest. Not satisfied with the display, two of the others grabbed legs from each side, then combined their efforts to at first rock forward and back, then fling the carcass far from the stage over the heads of the stunned onlookers. Adding to the bizarre effect, they then mimicked and parodied its landing with an embarrassing thud directly atop the incoming townsfolk already pressing hard to the front. Still not content with the effect of their antics, or the crowd's subdued reaction, they had the village simpleton return and for a handful of silvers, he gleefully agreed to be thrown from the stage himself, thinking, *"These strangers really seem to like me!"* This sorry attempt at engaging the spectators may have worked in their own pompous world, but here, few understood the display as anything other than a twisted mockery. None who witnessed took it kindly, and as to being engaged ... no ... they were not. To the crowd's collective dismay, the simpleton then flew helplessly over their heads even as a cluster rushed about frantically, albeit unsuccessfully to catch and brace his fall.

He survived, probably a few broken limbs, possibly worse. In those times a likely death sentence for a simple pig herder, who until that moment of innocent curiosity and the enticement of reward, had been happy, satisfied, and fulfilled, loved by his family, and treated with dignity and respect by all who knew him. A mere child trapped in an adult's body, he had no clue as to the degree of evil in the hearts of others.

Master Li merely turned away from the spectacle and crossed his arms. He disapproved, and now they knew.

Town Headsman Liang San
calls all to the ready.

Know Your Enemies

Always, know your enemy! No less than the great sage of strategy, Sunzi proclaimed this among his essential rules for success in battle and engagement. "Know your enemies and yourself, you will not fail in a hundred battles. Know yourself but not your enemies, sometimes you will succeed, sometimes not. Know neither and you will be forever imperiled."

Li Fung knew himself, and he knew the heart of his enemies. As to the particulars, he trusted his instincts to figure them out on the wings of the unraveling moment.

The Knights of Wei well appreciated the cornucopia of blessings harvested from their hard earned talents, just as they cherished and held tightly to their esteemed and much envied positions. No trick, device, science, or art was spared in keeping them at the top of their game. Arrogance went with the role, why be modest when you were the best? Funny thing about arrogance though. The whole world sees it before you even have a clue it's already poisoned your essential nature.

The likes of Zhang Fei and Guan Yu and the others of
their epoch age might never be seen again. The special
cauldron which birthed them already lay in disarray. But
magicians, herbalists, bone crackers, physicians and
soothsayers had come a long way since then. Now, nothing
would be left to chance, or nature. What went into Wei's
Knights was studied systematically even as it came out their
rears. Diets were then modified, nutrients changed, organs
massaged and meridians stimulated, all under the directive
and full support of the imperial court. A new breed of
warrior emerged, and here stood their finest. How can
anyone compare them to what came before? Their instincts
were sublime, their strength unprecedented, their speed
beyond the imagination of those more ordinary. No one
knew where this started, or if it would ever end. Bigger,
better, faster, more deadly, now the constant mantras of
Wei's physicians and scholars. It made all of them quite
wealthy. Surely they could sense the outside world
withering under the fruit of their efforts?

As it were, the knights knew their status at court hinged
inevitably on ruthless displays of superiority, particularly in
instances such as this, requiring a quick dispatch of the
unimpressive specimen standing before them. Yes, they
might be arrogant. Were they not supreme? Simply remove
the hillsman from the circle. Send the required message.
Then get out. A deed no more daunting than any of the
thousands they had unflinchingly performed in the past.

They didn't know Li Fung, or if they did, they couldn't
remember, nor did they care to. The odds stood
overwhelmingly in their favor. That's what they knew.

They saw no further than the tips of their own noses. Each had made sure to wager unsparingly on the pre-ordained outcome. No harm in profiting, good for one's motivation. For an anxious moment or two, they debated hotly amongst themselves, but loud enough for all to overhear, over who would have the distinction of throwing the impudent bastard from the circle. Some astute observers in the crowd wondered. Was this really who they were? Or had even their debate turned somehow into part of a fabricated in the moment show?

Master Li thought only this, *"The Knights of Wei will have no 'play' at my expense, at least not today."*

Elegant simplicity.

Admirable.

The contestants staked positions within and around the circle. Li Fung, whose size and stature we've already noted, certainly taller than most by provincial norms, still seemed dwarfed by the court manufactured titans surrounding.

It does not surprise. The odds though already steep, now escalated even further against him.

"No matter", he thought as he heard the gamesmen still calling for bets in the crowd. He witnessed the knights passing purses of gold, not timid in the least, showfully staking their anticipated returns.

"I will do what I can do, I've no money to wager, and wouldn't if I did."

Unlike lowlanders, mountain folk disapproved of gambling. The lowlanders, particularly those of Fortune's Gateway, gambled incessantly. Perhaps that had something to do with their history of success in trade, while the world about them burned. The art of skirting disaster and harvesting profits amid uncertainty. Even the mountain folk admired the fluidity of the profiteers, and their abilities to play all sides in the heat and heart of each uncertain moment; balancing this and that, until the will of heaven finally clarified and drew them like moths to its glowing ember.

The moment neared, they all stood to the ready. Liang San bid for the attention of the contestants, ensuring they could see his every move, as also could the crowd and the witness scribe. He held the sandglass high and readily visible, no uncertainty, top side empty, bottom side full. As though slapping a cup after downing a draught, he struck his free hand hard and loud to the tabletop, then turned the glass over, calling "Kaishi (begin)!" for all to hear. And with that, he set the timer down before the scribe as the match commenced.

Li Fung did not know from where the first attack would come, nor did he know if it would come from one, or from all five. Luckily he glanced instinctively eastward. It had been drummed into him from childhood, "Keep center and listen. Face first to the direction of likely threat, on this day, the north, where stood the leader. Then beware of the east and west; and never forget the south." Precisely on the command to start, the Green Knight bridged from the east, closing the distance between with a spectacular leap. Both hands, more claws than hands, reached toward Li like grappling hooks.

They seemed sure to land and lock on their helpless prey, until the very last instant when Li Fung swung his right foot wide in a calculated rear-ward arc, leaving nothing but air for the Green Knight's now clumsy descent. Li Fung kept his hands low, and tucked, his opposite knee forward toward his opponent in a stance Shi-Hui Ke recognized as 'Opposing Dragon' a reflection of the essential first move. Allowing no pause, the Knight started to come a second time. Master Li sprung lightly like a grasshopper to the attacker's right rear, now using his own hands as grappling hooks. He would have called out "Panther" had this been a teaching session, and like a panther, he locked his fingers from behind onto both sides of the green giant's throat, pinching nerves, muscles and blood vessels with a closing grip so tight the giant stood paralyzed, reaching upward with his two arms gamely trying to pry loose as Li Fung broke his now distracted balance rearward and down. Though undoubtedly skilled, Green had never encountered anything like this in his Jiao Ji. Wherever he grabbed onto Li, the limb seemed to expand and grow mocking his effort and he could do nothing to lessen or to loosen it. Without stopping, now arcing his left foot to the rear, Li Fung coalesced spinning circle energy as he spiraled the Knight's head face downward, corkscrewing him into a brutal collision with the platform. Though it took a long moment, when Green finally lifted his head as though willing himself to rise, a lightning heel kick from Li Fung's right foot drove it down even harder into the unforgiving surface.

All were silent and stunned as the fallen giant remained motionless, presumably unconscious; possibly worse. Still in Panther, Li Fung took Green's position to the east and glowered menacingly toward the others.

To Liang San's relief, no blood. To his delight, several fragments of teeth, like bones of portent lay scattered about. *"Who could interpret their pronouncement?"*, thought the headsman. The scales of likely outcome now backstepped slowly from their precarious imbalance, to a point slightly removed from the abyss of no hope, but still some ways from equilibrium.

Liang San quelled the urge to beam in admiration and pride for Li Fung over what anyone in Wei's military aristocracy would have considered a stunning and humiliating upset. Fortunately, prudence and love of life kept the headsman in check.

Glancing to the sandglass, he thought, *"All accomplished in less time than it would take to pee."*

Li Fung turned to the other knights and requested, "Please remove him from the ring, or you will leave me no choice …"

Compassion, why waste a life for a contest, even the life of an enemy. Here, Li Fung's ledger had no need for tally, nor use for justice against an opponent already downed. Doing more would say nothing. At least not to him.

It was minister Long Hsieh who ordered the removal. Once removed, those in the crowd saw Long Hsieh cut away the knight's green tunic and throw it in disgust from the stage, a clear message for the remaining four, who, despite their sense of loyalty, could show no empathy for their fallen comrade, who, should he ever come to, would likely find himself shamed before all things Wei. Only in this brief lingering moment would he have some degree of oblivious safe harbor before entering upon his new life among the ordinary and expendable.

The point of such display by the minister? Had Sunzi been standing alongside him, he would have whispered disapprovingly, "Needless punishments only put your own distress on a golden platter for all to relish. Proportionate to the severity of the reaction, nothing changes but for your enemy confirming the degree his actions have wrought your distress. Let loss and failure be their own opinion. Those things can be rectified easily enough, provided you demonstrate unerring loyalty and dedication to your purpose."

The other knights could only wonder, *"What will become of him, if and when he comes to?"* For this, they had no answer, except to look with more determination toward Li.

A Life's Purpose Revealed

Now, as impatient onlookers urged for the match to continue, distress and uncertainty nibbled at the minister, perhaps even infecting his knights.

They had work to do. Get past this setback. Take care of business! Only in that could they restore their dignity and overcome this unfortunate distraction.

Taking care of business. In that regard they were true kin to Li Fung.

The remaining four knew their roles, it would next be the White and the Red who entered the circle, from the west and the south. Red embodied Yang in full bloom, symbolized by the Vermilion Bird emblazoned over the broad crest of his gilded tunic. On the coat of his partner, a White Tiger, hinting at new Yin, and perils unseen until loosed when least expected.

Reading their intent, Master Li backed to the northeast quadrant, where he could keep both in full view, and work their sides, should one or the other move forward, being ever mindful of Black and Yellow still threatening from the north and southwest. Black and Yellow, standing outside the circle, held their intentions for good reason. Should Li Fung break angle on either of their two partners, his trajectory would place him within strike or reach of whichever of the remaining two stood nearest. Maybe an oversight in the lay of the rules, maybe not; there was no declared caveat against their reaching in from the outside and pulling Li from within. At the very least, it would distract Li enough that one of those inside might deliver the crippling strike to newly exposed openings. So they had planned.

Red moved first. He closed from the south in a mad dash peaked by a series of lightning kicks, pokes and slashes. All four extremities moving independently, having minds of their own, edging forward like threatening blades, giving no stay or opening for Li to counter. Truly, the spirit of Yang radiating in all its dimensions.

Li Fung considered first to angle North, then saw the Black Knight staring invitingly, almost as if he had read the thought. Li remained unfazed. Rather than engaging the charging Red, or crossing toward the waiting White where he would then be completely surrounded, he elected to do the unexpected. Attack Black! Disable their leader! And with that, he sprung toward the Black Knight, but only so close as to spit. The glob of spittle sailed straight and centered at the head knight's startled expression. Luckily he closed his mouth! Though Black knew to hold his ground, his instinctive revulsion trumped reservation, causing his upper body to involuntarily dip left down and away from the disgusting projectile. *"I will make Li pay for this"* raced through his mind. During the barely perceptible instant it took for that thought to cross Black's awareness, Li Fung stepped to the very edge of the circle with his lead leg. The agreed rules said he had to be removed from the circle, they said nothing about whether he could step one foot out, leaving the other anchored within. You see, rules, like all laws and constructs, can be interpreted, even twisted or bent any which way we choose, so long as we carefully mine the details, and work them accordingly. They were doing it, weren't they? Why couldn't two play this game! With that, his right foot stepped far outside the circle, bringing him nearly eye to eye with Black, whose raised head and stunned look only added to the crowd's delight and then unmitigated awe when both of Li's fully extended arms delivered the 'Gift of Wind' to the giant's ears. This variation of 'Boxing the Tiger's Ears' meant simply that Master Li cupped air in his palms, and clapped them with all his now rooted energy directly over the giant's ears. Unless you have some experience of this bitter wind rattling about inside your skull, you may not fully appreciate the agony of the Black Knight as he screamed, and dropped to his knees, with rivulets of blood trickling like miniature falls over lobes on both sides. Mind you, he wasn't yet finished, though true, he would not ever hear again. For the moment, as with East, North no longer threatened.

Minister Long Hsieh called loudly, "Foul, he stepped from the circle! We have won!" and was immediately shushed by an annoyed Liang San who answered, "I saw no fouls, all were yet within the rules. Li Fung's left leg still held root within."

Liang San wished Fa Miu had been with him when the ground rules were set. The fox could smell controversy from a distance and knew well how to avoid it. *"Damned details! Give them a fingernail, they'll take the whole arm!"*

Master Li had been sure to keep White, the white tiger, within peripheral view all this while. As birthing yin, and much unlike Red, White held steady, looking only for the lethal strike, knowing the opening would come before long. It always did! Patience! One of the fundamental principles of warfare reminded how doors and windows were certain to open and close when conditions changed, and sometimes when opened even a fraction, a bit of audacity went a long way. Here's the rub. The timing simply could not be easily predicted, though as tiger, White knew patience to be the virtue which tricked locks on nearly all opportunities. Nature dictated the necessity of faults and imperfections, no matter how strong or formidable something might at first appear. Their inevitable presence facilitated needed change, and birthed variation, within which all potentials found their root. Within nature's ever evolving manifestations, they occurred freely, and timed themselves as only they deemed fit. One could puzzle over whether this benefited the many creatures, in whose midst these maddening oscillations unfolded in constant challenge to their very existence. As tiger, the White Knight judged it wise to know of them, and to master their myriad nuances to great advantage.

Li understood the animals, and knew how they thought. That primal knowledge stood innate, coming for him long before, and beginning in childhood onslaughts of thoughts, experiences and philosophies wherein eventually emerged what we might think to be the martial arts. For him, something more visceral. He would say this awareness of animal movement came to all of us, as it did him, a birthright. He couldn't explain it convincingly to skeptics, nor was he inclined to waste time trying. Those who doubted questioned, "How does one acquire knowledge and skill, without experience?" But he knew it as fact, already there and in place before the experience. Humankind consolidated the lessons of its trials, achievements, and failures en masse, assimilating all it had seen, survived and surveyed in its coursing through life, challenge and eternity. The animals moved within us, all of them. Their images, instincts, and inclinations served as metaphors, each one a key unlocking some vast potential. In fact everything that had ever been already lay preserved for us, just beneath that flimsy ripple of reality we think of as our world. There, in their lair, our lair, poised and ever ready to race to our beckon. We were, after all, animals ourselves. We only needed reach and summon to where they stood, ever ready to turn the scales about on our uncertain moments.

Knowing this, Li realized the principle of openings could not always be relied upon. Nothing was infallible, not even for the wary and patient tiger. More than anyone would expect, what the tiger thought to be his ultimate advantage could as readily cut against the grain of opportunity, as with it. You see, when scouring for openings against your opponent, you sometimes lose view of those within yourself. This, Li knew far better than others. Neither potential could exist without the other. The intent to initiate attack is already an opening, a vulnerability.

One thing stood for sure in this sliver of time. When last seen, Red closed fast upon Li's rear. He pursued to close his kill even as Li delivered the gift of wind to Black. Unbeknownst to Li, Red had already begun his iron palm strike toward Li's thoracic spine, looking to instantly paralyze him by severing his root via the neural cord. Once Li lay crippled and motionless on the ground, the others would be free to extract their due, reciprocating with defilement and humiliation fair recompense for their fraternity's public rebuff.

Li Fung harbored no lust for vengeance. For him, such thoughts were only complications best avoided. Distractions. He reckoned there was a reason for his existence, and his accumulation of broad experiences over a humble lifetime. Bolstered by unending tests, none of which brought him joy or peace, he now saw they all led simply to this spot, and this single moment. Until this day, he had not known his supreme life's purpose. Survive this match! By acting with uncompromising righteous intent, it fell to him, and no others, to show the Wei usurpers for what they truly were. Simple as that!

Li understood the geometry of flow. It's there you know, whether you see it or not. Most can't, so don't feel left out. Mind you, it's not easy to explain how this works. When one understands the topology of flow, one begins to see things even before they happen, sometimes even before they are thought to happen. Some refer to this as "listening" but for those in the know, "listening" and "seeing" stand completely apart. I would caution, don't take literally what follows; just accept the truth of it. Though Li physically stood listening within the circle, snakelike threads of his awareness remained ever apart, in this case rising upwards oscillating in the atmosphere above, and staring down to events below, taking all in and giving due study. That awareness read only one opening against Li in the particular moment. The events preceding, and the constraint of the circle left just his spine open, and for that, only Red had access. Not even seeing the incoming strike, Li knew to angle left and as he turned, to go to ground with a right shoulder roll directly over the character 'Shu' scribed mid circle. Hesitate and all would be lost! He completed a full roll, with an increasingly frustrated Red still in hot pursuit. White now saw the anticipated vulnerability as Li completed his roll ending left side down only to glimpse the white tiger, already airborne and about to drop upon him. Li knew to flow like water, no time for thought, simply let the body do what it would, keep the mind out of it. And with barely the time to move, he went flat on his back and raised his folded right leg, pointing the ascending knee directly at White's descending torso. They met with a loud crack of introduction, which Li knew to be the sound of a sternum splintering. *"Pleased to meet you"*, thought Li Fung as White dropped helpless off to Li's right; and with that, Li disengaged, log-rolled hard left, then popped up as monkey standing to the ready, squaring on Red with Yellow outside the circle behind him.

The scribe called for all to hear, "We are at the half point!"

Long Hsieh glared back, as though implying impropriety in the keeping of time, "So Soon?"

Black, still reeling in pain rose cautiously to standing, trying to find his balance and his bearings, White couldn't breathe beneath his split sternum, nor could he stand; his desperate sucking for air drew empathy even from those in the crowd who despised the Wei. You'll find it true, even callous merchants scouring for opportunities may yet have little tolerance for blatant suffering in their midst. It's one thing to hear about it from over there, quite another to have it staring you directly in the face.

The Wei attendants discretely removed the second fallen knight from the ring, beneath the mounting rage of Long Hsieh whose face seemed to be boiling uncontrollably.

Yellow now stood to the ready. By signal, Long Hsieh motioned for Red to stand down.

Boy Meets Fox

From the roof to the west, little Shi-Hui Ke peered carefully, weighing what he had witnessed, thinking only, *"Have I missed the thought cutting? Was it in there somewhere? What am I supposed to be looking for? Where is this thought which cuts? How will I answer if Master asks me to describe what I saw? Oh! Who's to say any of this matters anymore. We'll likely be pig's fodder by day's end."*

Just then, a noise emanating from the street below drew the child's attention. While the crowd in the plaza focused on the Yellow Knight about to engage Master Li, Hui, like a turtle, pushed his head and neck out and cautiously over the roof's edge to see what might be going on below.

In the ways adjoining, he saw a group of men pushing through the crowd, now and then grabbing for the attention of adjacent shop owners, at times even pointing to the building where he lay, as though asking questions about the structure. No one seemed to have any answers. Most just shrugged their shoulders and shook their heads, then politely steered away.

"What are they looking for?"

Young Hui noted the men were all armed, and wore the colors of Wei. He saw no town constables, and found it puzzling. Soldiers of Wei had no formal authority here. Why were they unescorted and acting so rude as that?

"Bullies," he thought.

After some considering, the child decided it did not concern him. He slid back to his vantage point looking expectantly toward the stage in anticipation of what might follow, and ever minding the possibility he might yet have to help his teacher.

But just as he positioned at his lookout, a hand grabbed his shoulder from behind.

Still prone, and frozen by the unexpected, he turned his head and saw a man whose face he remembered from below and whom he recognized only from casual sightings during walks about town with his people. He would hear expressions like, *"There he is, Liang San's right hand"; "Townsfolk say he administers fairly"; "He knows everything, and pulls the unseen strings"; "He can be crossed only at great risk. Best to keep him as an ally."*

Hearing these things made the child curious but wary, at least to the extent he once prodded Master Li Fung and pointing, asked "That man there, I hear others talk of him in ways uncertain. He sounds to be powerful, but he looks and walks about like a street merchant, only with nothing to do or sell."

"Yes child. Some say he is powerful. I can't say one way or the other. This town changes current often, and it's hard to say who is really what. I do know he administers under the authority of Headsman Liang San, and those over whom he administers consider him a great improvement over his predecessors."

"What else do you know?"

"Only that many call him 'Fox' when his back is turned, though his name is Fa Miu. I think there may be a reason for that."

"Do you like him?"

"I do not know him well, but if I did, I think I would indeed like him."

"How can you know that?"

"It simply seems to me that he and I walk with the same wind blowing to our backs."

"What does that mean, Master?"

"Ah, little one, so many imponderables. So hard to explain. Best to simply trust you will know when you have the need."

And for little Hui, that moment was now.

He looked hard to the face behind the hand on his shoulder, seeing a figure crouched carefully alongside, clearly also not wanting to be seen from below.

"You are Fa Miu, what do you want with me?" yelled the boy.

"Child, keep your voice down. Carelessness will draw the attention of others."

"Others?"

"You saw them, did you not? The soldiers of Wei below?"

The boy answered, "I have nothing to do with them. I did nothing wrong."

"There's no time for explanations, I've come to ensure your safety."

"My safety? No one even knows I'm here. Who sent you?"

"Li Fung sent me, he knew you'd be at risk if found out."

"Found out?"

"Yes, the Wei know you're here and come for you now as we speak. They want you desperately, and if possible, will exploit you to defeat or destroy Li Fung."

"How do I know you're not with them? Master Li would have told me about you, or given some sign."

Silence. Then Fa Miu thought for a moment, "*A sign? Yes, Li would have given a token to show I could be trusted.*"

Then Fa Miu nodded knowingly, "Your name, I could not possibly know it but for Li Fung having given it to me. You are Shi-Hui Ke. He told me I would do well to remember your name, and now it appears I have."

Shi-Hui Ke mulled on this for a moment. There were no other options. His hideaway had been found out. He reasoned if Fa Miu were an enemy, he would already have shown his true colors. "*Besides, he could only have learned my name from Master Li, who would only have given it to someone he trusted.*"

Only one question remained.

"How did you know to find me here?"

"I saw you when I stood with Li Fung, and let him know as much. I too thought you would be safe, but then I saw Minister Long Hsieh dispatch his thugs, and took it upon myself to investigate. Indeed, a shopkeeper below confirmed they seek a boy wearing Shu mountain garb. That meant only you, and triggered my promise to Li Fung. And so, I am here."

Now fully convinced, young Hui bowed, "I thank you in advance for your assistance kind sir. What would you have me do?"

"We stay put, for now. Any movement on our parts will only risk giving away our position. With luck they may still lose themselves on false trails. The shop keepers below will not give us up."

Hui asked, "Can we watch what remains of the challenge?"

"Of course," and with that, both Fa Miu and the child dropped prone to the rooftop, peering cautiously through openings in its rampart toward the stage.

The Phoenix Rises

Now, in the midst of contest, Li suddenly felt very alone. For a moment, he worried instinctively over the boy. He felt distracted by his concern, but couldn't dismiss it. He then stared briefly about looking for Fa Miu, only to see what appeared to be him hurrying westward from the plaza, following close behind a squad from Wei. He couldn't know for sure what it meant, but he guessed the child had been found out. Could he trust Fa Miu?

If not Fa Miu, then who? In that moment, he grew despondent. Mountain folk knew this feeling well, and within themselves kept a place for it. It can be like that you know. What joy and fulfillment they might derive from each other, their culture, or their community high in the clouds always stood under threat of imminent end. They governed treacherous passages which might make, or break empires. At least that's what others thought. For the tribespeople, simply a home. Nothing else compared, so they stayed, and bore the consequences. But still, the thought of someday losing it in spite of all they and their forbears had sacrificed festered like an open wound. What would become of them if they had nothing?

Among the oppressed, such despondency can incline toward madness; especially when it comes upon you because of your existential reality. Things completely removed from your control. Simply there, close by, always. It's best to find a place for such gloom. Lock it up. Put it where you can keep an eye on it. That's what they did. That's what Li Fung would do now, if he might just once again remember how. Stress can steal your focus, and cause you to irretrievably lose track of even yourself.

Ah, here it is, the formula returns. *"Take charge."*

With that, Li Fung let go his concerns, and remembered to trust his instincts. They had never failed him in moments like this. Always, his one safe harbor. His sanctuary.

Already knowing from where next attack would likely come, he turned to southwest, smiled politely, and respectfully issued his dragon bow as overture and invitation to the Yellow Knight. The still fresh Yellow had hoped Li would by now be showing some signs of wear, or even tiredness, but he saw no such thing, *"Why, the bastard isn't even breathing hard."*

"A challenge for you sir!" called Li Fung to the Yellow Knight.

Yellow wore the embroidered Yellow Dragon on his tunic. This spoke of balance and harmony between the Yin and the Yang, and also to the consummate skill of the wearer. The color Yellow had been reserved, by nothing less than imperial decree, for only the most powerful and physically gifted of Wei's knights. He stood senior to Red for a reason.

"One suitable to a noble of your prominence," continued Li.

"Speak your piece!" replied the knight.

"Time is running!" called an exasperated Long Hsieh, only serving to draw a fearsome glare from his would be champion.

"We will trade strikes, nothing held back, here before all, each will stand directly in turn before the other. If you knock me from my feet, you win. If I knock you from your feet, I win. Since this is my proposal, I will respect courtesy and allow you the first hit."

Why would Li do this? Doesn't it seem foolish? Perhaps he was indeed exhausted and pretending otherwise, or could it yet be the boy, still weighing on his concerns?

No one thought Li could out muscle, or out strike the Yellow Knight. Therein lay the bait. A proposal too enticing to summarily dismiss. For Li, it echoed again how he drew them into the game in the first place. Wave your concession before them, subject it to a test where they saw no chance of failure. Simply irresistible.

Or then again, maybe there too is a bit of the fox in Li Fung.

It is said if you encounter a stranger in the marketplace who wagers a sovereign gold piece he can pull a phoenix from his naval, you should never take the bet. If he gives you favorable odds; two to one; three to one; ten to one; reject the offer all the more firmly!

"Why?" you ask.

Because in a convincing and indisputable fashion, he will in some way, some how pull ashes from his naval and from those ashes a phoenix will rise under your very nose. As you stare in disbelief, hopes of quick riches dashed, the stranger will walk merrily away with your gold piece, dropping it into the same purse where many others already lay.

Seeing the sandglass running, and not countenancing further interference from Long Hsieh, Yellow quickly nodded his assent. No fool, he knew even if he failed to knock Li Fung to the ground, the hillsman would doubtless be so weakened by the first strike as to render his own attempt at counter futile. So, that became Yellow's plan for the moment. Flatten him, or grind him down; then fling what remained to the four winds.

Wasting no time, he dropped to a rear favored bow position locking his huge break hardened right fist to his already turned pelvis. He then lifted his left hand to ready, and Li Fung politely stepped forward smiling his warm smile, fearlessly pressing his chest up and against the tips of Yellow's pointed left fingers, positioned mid air to act as rangers gauging and measuring for his strike.

"This may be too easy," thought Yellow. He had learned from thousands of repetitions how to shift smoothly from rear bow to forward bow, all resistance purged from his technique, and to drive his hammer-hardened right fist like the head of a rabid ram through any object in its path. He had so finely tuned the motion it would flow instantly, no sooner thought to begin than ended, all targets pulverized. On the field of combat, many had attested to his 'iron fist' and marveled at how it ripped through the chest plates and battlefield armor of enemy chieftains. Even when it failed to penetrate the armor, the unfortunate recipient might find the very protection he had worn to repel such blows, had turned inward, like a crushing hull mashing through soft tissue behind. Either way, once struck, dead where they stood. None could escape. Yellow had proven this countless times in battle, and in challenges. Not surprisingly, he had lost count of those he killed this way; once past fifty, the faces all blended together and became indistinguishable. By then, simply a blood sport he had mastered and had no further feeling about. He didn't go out of his way to do this. The situation simply presented, and he acted to ensure his own survival, and status. Knights learn early, emotions get in the way, damnable compassion tails too closely to their beckon and makes only for complications.

"But this wily fellow moves like lightning. I must be sure to execute perfectly, and deliver my judgment faster and more cruelly than ever before. It will be a worthwhile exercise for me, I'll use it to remove the dust from my technique. Who knows, I might even work up a sweat."

As a courtesy reciprocated for Li's taking first blow, Yellow waited for Li's nod of readiness, after which he would be free to unleash his fury.

All witnessed the nod.

No sooner had Li's eyes lifted than the yellow giant launched his killing strike.

The Thought Cuts

The move exploded from stillness, the rear bow shifting to forward and as it did, the rearward hip pivoted toward front, acting as chassis for the iron fist now rocketing toward its target like a battering ram.

What those on stage saw amounted to little more than a blur, followed by a thunder like clap announcing the strike had done its deed.

But had it?

The end of the fist stood visible over the spot where Li Fung had just been standing. Only, Li had turned and pivoted from his right. So fast had the two moved that the bewildered crowd had to let their minds catch their racing eyes before they all realized the punch had missed its target, though it cracked the wind like a whip lashing to extension. To everyone's astonishment, most of all, the Yellow Knight's, Li stood untouched and unharmed, his face expressionless.

Long Hsieh again called "Foul! He failed to take the strike!" already grabbing at Liang San's arm to demand justice.

Confounded, Liang San had been caught off guard by Li's masterly evasion. The words of Li's original challenge replayed through his mind but before he could weigh them to conclusion and address Long Hsieh, the Yellow Knight turned to his principal and spoke for himself, "He has the right within the challenge to evade, if able to."

That silenced the minister, who released his grip from Liang San, saying nothing more.

"Thank the stars he spoke up. I was at a complete loss on how to rule." raced through Liang San's mind.

Never before having seen such a display of complete emptiness, the Yellow warrior could only smile over his own frustration and the miracle he had witnessed. He knew what just happened had been beyond his control. He didn't believe it, but he knew it. And the reality pulled a smile from his still determined jaw and tightened lips. Witnessing something like this can only be appreciated for what it was, even if it crossed one's own purpose.

"My turn," said Li.

Yellow had not banked for this, but then again had on past occasions taken full hits from far more impressive warriors; and still fared well even afterward. His confidence remained unshaken.

The challengers squared off, now it remained for Li to strike the Yellow Knight. As did Master Li, the Yellow Knight walked directly to his opponent's front, bared his enormous chest, then staked his rooted feet.

Once positioned securely before Li, he signaled his readiness to proceed.

From the rooftop, Fa Miu whispered, "Watch closely boy!"

"It's done for us," said Shi-Hui Ke, "Master Li has great technique, I've no doubt; but he can't punch like that monster. Look at them. Don't be surprised if Master Li breaks his arm hitting that giant hunk of jerky."

Fa Miu laughed aloud, "True, but Li's thought can cut. It's sharpness can pass through any opponent, even that giant piece of jerky known as the Yellow Knight."

"You know the thought cuts?"

Fa Miu answered, "A bit, my young friend. But Li Fung, if rumors among the outliers can be believed, has mastered it."

"Tell me, what is it?"

"Watch boy, and you will see for yourself."

The boy muttered to himself, *"Is it possible there is no such thing as a plain answer to any of my simple questions? Why do I even ask them?"*

"I will use Ji[14] to move you" declared Li, as he stepped momentarily back and ran the sequence several times in the air, setting his left hand forward, drawing back the right hand, raising it, almost letting it float on its own, then with his entire relaxed body pivoting forward with the hand, all moving as one, almost as though every molecule, every atom of his torso aligned momentarily on the same governing axis and rotated in unison, his right hand delicately making contact with the left and the two gliding effortlessly forward, floating out and up, then disconnecting and drifting apart, finally relaxing to his side.

Those in the crowd turned to one another, asking, "What the hell is he doing?"

Most shrugged their shoulders, "Not a clue. Maybe he's lost his mind."

Some elders in the crowd recognized the movement. It had long been regarded as one of the eight essential energies, beneath which all postures and movement worked as launching platforms. Mastery of the esoteric energies required great dedication and reflection over spans of years to unlock their deep secrets. In troubled times, opportunities for such dedicated practice simply did not exist, and regrettably, for that very reason, the high arts receded from fact into legend. As a practical matter, everyone knew this and accepted the reality, preferring to no longer waste time

---

[14] "Ji," one of the previously noted essential energies defining the internal arts. It means "to press," but signifies much more, as you will see with what unfolds.

in the pursuit. Most doubted such skills ever existed in the
first place, and felt chasing after them simply diverted
energy and time from techniques more quickly learned, and
already proven by hard trial to be lethal and effective. In
that particular age, survival today always came first, out of
necessity. Skills gained tomorrow could well leave you dead
today. So, pondering the imponderables had become an
unaffordable luxury, a distraction; fodder for the dreamers.
Who could argue against such sound logic?

Even though great warriors could be found on all sides,
they were usually chaps who mastered the ability to knock
each other down with channeled violence and brute force;
and not magic. Onto that they hitched the efficiencies of
modern weaponry, and the knowledge of elixirs and potions
which made their blood rage to their beckon. While the poor
starved, they gorged on meat and whatever else it took to
inflate their bodies, minds, and spirits to unprecedented
extremes of size, intensity and capacity for violence. Perhaps
not magic, but certainly wizardry of sorts.

Fortunately, most met their ends before having to bear
the irreconcilable tolls these choices taxed on their persons.

Li Fung came from a different time and place, a domain
where refinement of the inner self earned the respect and
admiration of peers. Already embedded in their remote
traditions and ways were the philosophies and lessons of
great masters; the usual ones of course, but we mustn't
overlook the added influence and fine tunings of Zhuge
Liang, Guan Yu, Zhang Fei and Colonel Sun, why even the
elusive Sying Hao might one day be counted among them.

So, you could say Li knew a thing or two about harnessing oneself to the back of a dragon and riding the unseen forces to the peak of their stunning manifestations. Magic, if you will.

"I hope you've come with more than that," jibbed the Yellow Knight, as he studied Li's several repetitions, admittedly wondering what Li intended to do. "Ji is a fine technique, in its proper place. With the stakes today, you might want something more promising."

Li of course didn't have to go through with his charade. He knew the technique just like he knew the nose on his face, and could have done it instantly, or at any moment. No fool, he too kept close eye on the sandglass. With his play, and his "showmanship" if you will, he was killing time, and recovering energy. As he did nothing in front of everyone, right under their noses he built such an atmosphere of suspense that no one recognized or objected to his ploy.

Except Fa Miu of course. It could not pass his fox's nose undetected. "Look boy, see how he spends their time, doing nothing but practicing grabbing the bird's tail, still keeping the interest of the crowd, even his adversary. He is a very clever fellow."

Shi-Hui Ke nodded as if hearing something he already knew well; but in fact, could not conceal the great pride and admiration his entire being now radiated for Li Fung. For him, Li was here for the Shu people, and by his actions had brought their very best right to town center for all to witness.

Li answered the Yellow Knight, "It will be enough. Please sir, confirm you are ready. Be sure to brace your best for my strike."

The knight re-checked his stance, doubly confirming all nine points of contact beneath each foot locked tightly to the ground. He checked his weight and distribution, then carefully exhaled three times, while descending his hands palm down from on high, pressing to earth and his root in what some might recognize as what eventually inspired the first breathing form of Ba Gua.

He nodded his readiness.

Li smiled politely, "Good ... now we go."

No surprises or trickery there.

In a sequence of moves matching what he had done earlier, only this time, so smoothly executed as to appear to be a single act ... let's be clear on this ... we're not talking speed, no explosions, no thrusts, no death screams, just a profound singularity of purpose starting when Li set his left foot forward. As his heel touched down and rolled to toe, his left hand lifted effortlessly to Ji platform position, just as his hips turned in and his right hand closed upon the left. Grasping the bird's tail. To someone in the crowd, it might have looked like that, the right hand moving toward an imagined bird in the left as though it were sneaking up and about to close on its phantom tail.

Then, at the last possible instant, the right palm snapped forward, driving itself into the left and with that, the combined unit sprang as though a mammoth stake bounced from the head of an enormous drum, hidden from everyone's view by the mist of Master Li's thought, from whence it reached out to cut deeply through whatever lay in its path. It contacted directly center on the Yellow Knight's exposed sternum. By appearances, no more than a touch. The knight had thought to evade, but until feeling the weight of impact, saw no threat, or reason to do so. By then, it was simply too late.

Long Hsieh cries "Foul!"

Treachery

Neither the crowd, nor those on stage were clear as to what happened. Most in the sea of expectant viewers still waited impatiently for Master Li to throw his best punch, and by now had tired thoroughly of his practiced simulations. Though they saw what they saw, they had no explanation for the Yellow Knight suddenly lifting upward from the platform and sailing from the ring, dropping hard toward ground only after slamming full body into Minister Long Hsieh. To no small degree of embarrassment, the minister stumbled uncontrollably backwards twisting every which way to regain his own balance. He was still flapping his arms in the air when he realized he had already departed the stage and was sailing clumsily earthward.

Like a cat, the Yellow Knight somehow managed to recover his balance before striking the ground. A close call perhaps, but inasmuch as honorable Yellow had miraculously recovered, Liang San could not rightfully rule he had been knocked from his feet, since in the end, he remained upon them.

Li took no issue with the determination. His satisfied expression confirmed he had made his point.

Of course Liang San apologized profusely on seeing how the townspeople made no effort to catch the minister, somehow agreeing through their own lines of unseen thought transference to simply let him bounce to ground.

Which he unceremoniously did. Revenge for the simpleton perhaps. The spread of his arms and legs, combined with the loud thud and grunt of impact seemed almost comical to those standing about. Though too polite to laugh at the misfortune of another, they were not so polite as to help him return to his feet.

That fell to Liang San, who jumped from the stage and personally lifted Long Hsieh to standing, then instructed his guards to guide the still shaken minister to his original post on stage. Headsman Liang San glared his displeasure at those in the crowd standing to the front, whispering thru clinched teeth, "You might have tried breaking his fall! What do you think would become of us if somehow he were seriously injured?"

"Like the pig herder?" spat one back in reply.

The scribe called out for all to hear. Time now stood at the three quarter mark. The end fast approached and the outcome still remained in doubt.

The Yellow Knight walked to circle's edge, barely stifling his grin at the minister's misfortune, frozen in the image of a featherless bird, flapping empty wings to no avail. He struggled to keep stone faced and morbidly serious in its stead. *"Actually, he did well, considering what might have befallen him"*, thought the warrior. He knew well the ferocity of crowds should they have opportunity to act without risk of discovery.

Master Li, understanding the knight's dilemma and seeing his struggle for self control, smiled politely, then respectfully looked away.

Since neither contestant had been downed, there could be no declaration of victory. The Yellow Knight, still stunned, numbed if you will, at the wonder of what he had seen and felt, also knew what he could never say, or smile at. The strike had nearly killed him. Another like it certainly would!

With the time announcement, little opportunity remained to defeat the Shu tribesman. Yellow could no longer leave anything to chance, or to the trust (now lessened) he had in his own skills. He quick scanned the area, confirmed Green and White remained incapacitated. Red, standing down as ordered, could scarcely hold his mark, fuming eager and ready to tear forward and finish his work. Their group leader, Black had finally risen to standing and recovered his senses, if not his hearing. With a nod, he confirmed full readiness, then in a sequence of hand signs recognizable only among the brotherhood, issued his orders.

They would now play their only option, treachery.

Like many of us, these knights tried to stand for something, when they could. Regardless of what double-dealing and deceit got them to where they were, once there, their altruistic inclinations re-engaged; actually, were ordered, to push forefront. They swore to codes of honor, loyalty, fraternity, and service which were exhibited by the imperial court as the highest standards of excellence and character for all to emulate. On first becoming a member of the exclusive brotherhood, a knight might struggle with the dichotomy of what he had been asked, even ordered to do to get there; then find he now had to repudiate such behavior as base, crude, primitive and uncivilized, particularly when it was done by others. Basically, it was what our enemies did, not us. All very confusing, but one need not look far to see traces of the same dichotomies radiating through the run of all human endeavors. The masses craved their deities. Believing such paragons existed in all their supposed purity and righteousness proved irresistible to the people and signaled for them where the will of heaven inclined. Fantasy! This has long been known to be the supreme set of reins. Deliver to the needy what they crave most. The imperial knights fit the bill perfectly.

Most knights knew exactly who and what they were, but carefully distinguished that from the practical importance of what others thought of who they were. As realists, they knew to buy into the big game. It didn't matter to them when the multitude subscribed to a fantasy. It only mattered that they, within themselves, knew exactly who they were at all times, and never got confused about it.

Stone, cold, killers!

On this point, the Yellow Knight had a bit of an issue. It seems some of the fantasy had somehow rubbed off on him.

Once out of the muck and the mire, he had thoughts of his own to push forward, even break free to be all he hoped he could be. A shining example for all! So he took the codes of honor, loyalty, chivalry, fraternity and service closer to his now aspiring to true righteousness heart. That may be why, of the five, he, and not the others, represented the delicate balance between yin and yang, and wore the Yellow Dragon. In his soul, he hoped to emulate the paragon of righteousness, Lord Guan. Yet, he also agonized over his failures, and the accommodations required of him. Often, he wondered if Lord Guan had to wade through the same horseshit, and make equivalent compromises born of necessity. His companions assured him Lord Guan, despite his reputation, was caught in the net no different than they, or any other imperial knight in having to conjure, weave and nurture a meticulous fantasy which by all accounts seemed to be what everyone wanted anyway. They were ever careful to remind him, in their business, it benefited no knightly fraternity to confuse the fantasy with the practical reality. Losing touch with reality put everything at risk for everyone.

So, Black had given his orders; and Yellow would have no choice but to obey, and once again gut his principles.

The plan called for Yellow to again stand position before Li Fung, and in accordance with the agreed challenge, administer his second blow. Red would hold position until Yellow moved, at which point he would close from the rear, and this time land his spine crushing twisting palm strike. As insurance, Black would come from the North with his 'Shashou Jian[15]'.

---

[15] The Assassin's Mace. Cloaked in mystery and fable. Considered by all who knew of it to be the supreme weapon.

The Assassin's Mace

The Assassin's Mace. To those seeing it for the first time, the weapon appeared quite normal. Nothing more than a weighted ball mounted atop a club, measuring less than an arm's length in total. To the unknowing, all too easy to underestimate. The Black Knight, consummately skilled at manipulation, kept it hidden on his person at all times. Only those closest to him knew it even existed, or where he kept it. Among the few privileged to know were his fellow knights. Now, in preparation for the end, he drew it from its tuck beneath the blood red wrap around his tunic, then carefully removed its hood. Uncovered, all that could be seen of it was a dark sphere, and ambient reflections from the pristine sheen off its highly polished surface, beneath which lay a sea of perfect darkness. The weighted ball had been rumored to be the remnant of a star or planetary body. Some thought a meteor. The other knights believed it to be jade, but had never seen jade of such color or caliber. A specimen of perfect roundness wherein one staring might see reflections, spirits, visions of the future, or one's own visage, though grossly distorted. Powerful tokens tended to act like that. According to legend, this particular stone first appeared in the Shang Dynasty, more than a thousand years before. We'll tell more of that at another time. The perfect sphere quickly drew the attention of shamans and soothsayers, both of whom had great influence during that period. From the beginning of time, wise men, and tricksters coveted such totems, knowing them to be portals to untold energies. It's properties were carefully recorded by those who previously experimented with and attempted to exploit and harness its secrets. Over the centuries, the body of knowledge grew and each successive holder tapped even deeper into its mysteries and its power. There seemed no end of possibilities.

Even back then, men secured high stature and position by banking in violence, then being willing to do what most would not to effectively engage it to their purpose. It should not surprise. This stone, rumored to be the mystical egg of a phoenix, soon enough drew the attention of those vying for ultimate control. From there it found its way directly into the hands of their most determined enforcers: the secretive Brotherhood of Assassins.

It remained in their control ever since, passing from master to disciple in a continuous line, until it ended in the hands of the Black Knight. You didn't hear about the Brotherhood of Assassins? Well, there are many such brotherhoods. Pinch yourself awake, and look about. They serve every society, every age, every belief. They have plagued existence almost from the beginning, and doubtless, will be there plaguing us as mankind rolls ever toward its long anticipated end. What makes them particularly perilous is our own irrational tolerance for their continued nefarious existence. Leaders convince us we need their valued services, tagging them as heroes or great unsung patriots; giving them extraordinary power over you know who. Us! Patriots? Maybe, maybe not. I tell you this. When you see the charred bodies of children and innocents, or experience the disappearance of neighbors or family members, or witness villages purged, crops poisoned and inexplicable illnesses spreading uncontrollably, you are perhaps so close as to already be drawing their unwanted gaze. Make quick your escape. Pray others will grant you haven and sanctuary.

Among the assassins, it has been recognized that only after coming into the hands of the Black Knight were the sphere's most sinister aspects finally unraveled. This was in no small part because of his own intuition regarding darkness, and his eagerness to push open its gates.

The stone captured energy, and did not ever let it go. Whatever went into the stone dropped into an eternity of emptiness, as though pressing through a cosmic veil which, once shut behind, precluded return, except perhaps as an occasional reflection of a lost and drifting soul, floating as a fleeting surface image to warn those viewing from the outside.

"Who could this have been?" they typically wondered, doubting at first what they saw, and what they thought they heard.

So when the sphere rolled the way of the Black Knight, it might have been a meeting par with the grand encounter of Guan Gung and Red Hare[16]. Except for the evil of course.

The Knight accepted it with a grim smile, knowing it secured his destiny. He never again let it part his person. Needless to say, at first, it played havoc with his concubines and associates, their curious touches and brushes with the orb sending them instantly across time and space to where they could never be found, or returned. Even Yama[17] and his demon hounds couldn't track them. Believe me, they tried. Seeing no purpose for the occasional spiritless bodies left behind as shells, the Knight had them cast to the flames, sparing them no further thought.

Sometimes, more during holidays and festivals, he would stew in his loneliness and stare into the orb. On occasion he might catch the fleeting countenance of one he had once known, even loved, peering through the veil accusingly.

Not all ghosts were forgotten. Not all ghosts forgot.

By the time it had passed to the Black Knight, his predecessors had already fashioned a mount worthy of its ominous stature, hence its taking on the appearance of and being called "mace." By then, it had touched many, and the play of reflections swirling endlessly on the surface usually

---

[16] Guan Gung's famed steed. inseparable in life, and in battle.

[17] Yama. Ruler of the underworld. Hell, if you will. Once, when confronted by the Creator for his evil doings, he defended himself eloquently, arguing to the Creator, "Hey … isn't this my job? Can you think of anyone who can do it better than me? Didn't you make me for this purpose? Forgive me sire, I fail to see the problem." Thus convincing the Creator, he earned his freedom and was freed to go about his business.

startled the other knights when they had the rare opportunity to glimpse it closely. The Assassin's Mace represented the quintessential essence, soul if you will, of their misguided fraternity, and it answered only to the most feared of knights who because of what he could do, demanded to be, and became in fact their leader.

The Black Knight wore the celestial tortoise embroidered on his tunic, and he represented full yin, counterbalancing Red's full yang. The Assassin's Mace represented a new and previously uncontemplated concept in weaponry. Complete absorption. It might steal your attention, drain your focus, weaken you, deplete you, entice you, attract you, charm you, or even turn you to dust. There could be no doubt. In the hands of the Black Knight, it could do these things, and so much more. If he wished, a mere touch would remove you permanently from the cycles of existence and the governance of karma. You would be gone. For good, no recourse, no hope. Aware only of what you have lost. None have ever come back. Their images flitting about its surface made clear their misery and their loss.

How did this come about?

For centuries, brilliant though ruthless and unprincipled men experimented with and tested the mace on infinite combinations and sequences of points along the governing nerves, meridians and blood vessels. Usually, these tests were conducted on unwilling volunteers, typically the elderly, the infirm, the indentured, the unwanted young or the poor. Close study was made of the consequences and effects under all conditions and even different times of day. At first, tests would involve robust strikes to places like the cranium, where few skulls could withstand the hardness of the jadelike sphere. Suffice it to say that from the first, a violent strike with the weapon could readily produce incapacitation or death. But it seemed capable of so much more, and one could not hold the stone without hearing its constant invitation, its beckoning to enter. That usually terrified the beholder to where most could bear to have nothing further to do with it. Some, however, not distressed by the enticement of evil, listened with whetted interest and probed, testing deeper and experimenting further. Over spans of time, their experiments became much more subtle and nuanced. Light and barely perceptible touches to specific points on the body were found to cause paralysis. Passing brushes to the clothing of strangers in the marketplace left them collapsing in agony after taking a few steps. A tap to a spot over the left brow would cause blood vessels to explode in the brain. A poke beneath the short ribs would stop breathing. Even the other knights feared and mistrusted the cursed thing. Judging by what they had seen of its use in the hands of their leader, its sinister nature was unfathomable. More than once, in the midst of the battlefield, while the knights fought for their very survival, Black would wave about his Assassin's Mace and choreograph a bizarre symphony of death. There he danced blissfully, hopping about like an ecstatic Kali fluttering this way and that, brushing, glancing, tapping, bumping and striking while countless bodies dropped, some in death, some in coma, some in agony, and some in the form of now useless containers for bones, blood, and echoes of life now lost, but without death's reprieve. Rarely did the others speak of it amongst themselves, words could not suffice to even quantify the degree of their horror.

One wonders what Guan Yu might have made of, or done with such a chap as this.

Make no mistake on this point. The Black Knight didn't oppress his comrades. Nor did he have need to threaten, coerce, or terrorize them. Silence did better than all of that. Silence, and then the occasional demonstration. Their terror driven allegiance secured, he had no need for tyranny. Even Yama steered clear of the infernal contraption. He didn't need another hell. One kept him busy enough.

It is believed the mace came to Black's possession by right of succession. First, as a young warrior, then as an apprentice, he had proven his worthiness time and again to his mentor and master. His own mind had been dark, as far back as he could remember, which wasn't far at all, since he usually acted without conscience or remorse, and found contentment only in the moment which, once ended, left him waiting patiently and in silence for the next. No frustrations, no anxiety; one needed the passage of time for such to manifest. In his dark and empty abode, time represented something in the thoughts of others, which to him clearly had no substance, and no practical use, simply another distraction.

A silver bullet? Hammer of the gods? Magic wand? Ultimate solution?

No … it's the Assassin's Mace. That's how we shall think of it; and that's how history remembers it, all the while casting doubt it ever existed. The apotheosized sinkhole of life's energy, able to steal creation's essence with little more than a tap. And what it confiscated, it never gave up. The ultimate agent for victory at all costs. A last resort, rarely shown, clouded in dark legend, used when all else failed.

Master Li Finds an Unlikely Ally

Fitting isn't it? Though each possessor would have you believe otherwise, the weapon could never willingly be surrendered by master to apprentice. Who would want to give it up? Always, it passed by theft, subterfuge and deceit, and only after the most trusted, if not formidable apprentice had somehow managed to seduce the heart of his (or her) teacher.

Walking with darkness gets lonely. Who can you trust once there. Confide in just one. That's the only chink in the armor it will take. Instantly, your precious treasure departs.

Do you not wonder about Guan's emptiness, and the Black Knight's emptiness. Can they be one and the same? If yes, then how and why could the men be so different, one supremely righteous, one not. Perhaps the answer lay in the vessel. Be sure to look closely at that before spinning to conclusions. Someone twisted from their core can seldom be turned straight and true, not even if you bless them with time, and your trust.

Li Fung knew instantly. Something was up, but he didn't know what. He scanned the stage carefully, but could see no change except for Black now standing. As he positioned before the Yellow Knight, he noted the unmistakable cloud of sadness weighing over his demeanor. It hadn't been there moments before. Master Li looked straight to his face. He had seen this look many times before. The funeral stare. On tending to the loss of a loved one, or an innocent child, or more often, friends killed in action, one could look only this way, there could be no hiding it. Usually reserved for those already dead, sometimes what we feel becomes so strong, it washes over all our attempts at dissemblance and speaks our truth in the single moment for all to see. Seeing the Yellow Knight's sincerity, and having witnessed his integrity, Li knew he had earned his counterpart's honest respect, and perhaps to some small degree, his esteem. Sorrow weighed in Yellow's face, in spite of all efforts to conceal it. All rooted in what he knew stood poised to happen. Li would be assassinated, and Yellow could not prevent it. Worse, his treachery would be part of it. He had no control over what would follow. Disgusted with his predicament, he agonized over how he would go forward with guilt over the death of this good man forever nailed to his conscience. He saw his only choice now to be the call of duty, and acting out his ordained role. Forget self, values, and even honor. All deeds must be played to their inevitable contemptible conclusions. Conscience had become a luxury beyond his purchase.

As before, Li walked directly to where the Knight held his lead hand forward, having stepped again into his bow position his striking hand now at the ready, and primed.

Li set his feet, and prepared to issue his nod.

He smiled warmly, "I truly enjoyed our play today, perhaps even more so because of your clever ricochet off of Minister Hsieh. Thank you for that humorous touch. And then somehow preserving your balance at the very last moment, a subtle feat only within the skills of a select and very capable few. I commend you. Oh, and you took my death strike very well. Hopefully, we'll both survive this final exchange, and final victory will not prove excessively costly to whoever wins, or loses."

The Knight nodded and blinked every so lightly in resigned agreement.

The scribe stood and called for all to hear, "The end fast approaches!"

Minister Long Hsieh screamed, "Hurry, the end is near; do what you have to do!"

His unexpected yell drew Li's attention just as he thought to nod his already raised head. He turned curiously looking to Long Hsieh's outburst, only to find his eyes were riveted not on his Yellow champion, but rather on a line to the North, where Li knew the Black Knight to be standing, there, but out of view.

"Treachery!" thought Li. *"Of course, it is their way."*

On the rooftop, Fa Mui nudged Shi-Hui Ke, "Look, trouble!"

"Where? I see nothing?"

"They've set a trap, and Li Fung doesn't have a clue!"

"Where? What trap?"

"Look closely boy, and learn. The Yellow Knight stands true, as agreed. He serves to distract Li from the treachery to his rear. I liked the chap. It's hard to believe he'd have a hand in this. The Red Knight no longer stands down, but now appears postured to strike, and the Black Knight ... Wait! What's that in his hand? No! This goes beyond imagination!"

Fa Miu had heard rumors of its existence, but had never quite bought into the likelihood of an Assassin's Mace. He figured the deeds of the Black Knight had been carefully spun into intimidating narratives by the historians and revisionists of the court. They knew from experience how fear of the unknown worked all for the better, if the unknown might be perceived as a reality. Hence, the purported Assassin's Mace. Indeed, he had heard of it and on hearing, attempted to learn whatever he could, but ultimately found nothing but tales, rumors, and hearsay, proof enough of its manipulated fabrication over doubtful substance. What made him most suspicious were the reports only one such instrument supposedly existed, and it could never be replicated. Why so? A gift from the gods? It had rarely been seen. Most only knew of it from rumor or report of others. As far as he knew, if it existed, whoever controlled it kept it close hold at court. Those who witnessed its use were usually its intended victims. Few had anything further to say about it. They wanted no part of it, nor did they want to tempt its anger. Fa Miu had heard only of a mysterious black orb used as a club which could suck the life from even a stone. He laughed the first time he heard this, "That's simply too much for a skeptic like me to bite into."

Hearing Fa Miu's concern, the boy abandoned precaution and stood tall along the roof's edge, looking desperately for what caught Fa Miu's attention. He saw Red. Nothing changed there. He remained ferocious, but wait, the Black Knight now had something in his hand, some type of wand. Shi-Hui Ke could see the sheen off its tip.

"The wand, you're concerned about the wand? Why it's nothing. Even if it were an iron topped mace, Master Li could manage it easily."

"Boy, Master Li stands before the Yellow Knight, naively trusting Wei will abide by the rules of engagement he set for the contest. It's my belief Black is holding the Assassin's Mace, a terrible weapon straight from the darkest bowels of hell. If legends be true, its mere touch will sap one's soul!"

The boy studied all carefully, measuring distance, running timing, seeing all possibilities, then uttered, "If the Yellow Knight attacks, Master's doom stands certain."

Fa Miu looked at first questioningly to the boy, then his own mind raced through the possibilities, closing its pursuit only when he saw Hui's deduction to be correct. Still, regardless of what the Yellow Knight did, Li's lot now lay bare and exposed to the imminent touch of death. Or worse.

"Well reasoned child, my fear is the Assassin's Mace. Li cannot risk even a touch while it remains in the hands of the Black Knight."

"Then there's no hope."

"Yes, one hope only, and I think you already know what that is."

The answer jumped immediately to his lips. There could be only one answer, "The thought cuts!"

Fa Miu nodded somberly. Now even he stood, as did everyone in the town, including the pursuing squad from Wei, stretching necks so as not to miss a thing. All attention riveted on the circle of combat. *"It would be his only chance of surviving the Assassin's Mace."*

Li Fung stood in a hopeless quandary. If he went ahead with his match against the Yellow Knight, he would be exposed to attack from the rear and side. Yet he could not give his back to the Yellow Knight and turn to the others. Seeing where they stood, he knew any change to face one, would expose him to two from the rear. He had no options, but to purge all thought and concerns from his mind, and to continue into oblivion, preparing himself to seize any opportunity which arose. Ah yes, strike instantly, when the opportunity presented. Somewhere, somehow, in the coming moments he must find a way to be very, very clever.

Yellow stilled before moving, he would not explode like the last time, but instead would stall; trusting the back beat would throw Li's remarkable timing off. Li, who usually put his focus on an opponent's midsection ("you really can't move anywhere without moving it first") for once, looked elsewhere, staring directly into Yellow's eyes. He hadn't noticed before, they were a remarkable shade of gray, tinged with yellow blue lines. To his surprise, they did not meet his gaze, but rather seemed to measure the horizon behind Li's head, as though Yellow were trying to see everything before him, panning left to right.

Only then did Li pick up on it. A gift from a new friend! At first barely a ripple in the reflection from one eye, but then the hint of a flicker, a movement; something that shouldn't be there, but was, now bouncing from both eyes, a movement from behind. Given the angle, it could only be the Black Knight. His final words to the Yellow Knight, just before nodding readiness to commence were, "One moment, Sir."

Fire!

And with that, Li stepped right foot fast to forward, nearly treading on Yellow's exposed lead foot, barely eluding Red's head crushing axe kick from the blind side. He lifted his left and pivoted 180 degrees angling just in time to see Black descending in quick follow-up with what appeared to be a massive, perfectly shaped black pearl, mounted on some sort of shaft. He had never seen the likes of it. Beautiful beyond measure. Though he turned to engage, he froze and stared, entranced by its spell, stuck where he stood while Black, in what was clearly a non threatening extension of the object, seemed to be reaching out to give Li an even better study of its beauty. From deep within Li, a need arose, so strong he could barely resist, *"I must touch the orb. I must touch the orb! So smooth and perfect, and empty beyond measure. I can be safe there, my many troubles will be left behind."*

No fool, the Red Knight knew to steer clear of the mace. Allowing the game now belonged to Black, he retreated to the ready.

Fa Miu looked on in horror from the roof, witnessing Li's left hand reaching for where the orb floated midway between him and the Black Knight. The knight stood patiently, waiting to deliver the "gift" of its touch. Li neared timidly, almost childlike, spellbound, entranced in innocent wonder over its mysterious beauty.

Fa Miu looked down. He could watch no more, he reached about to turn the boy's eyes away from the tragedy imminent, but the boy wasn't there.

A quick scan of the roof found the child precariously balanced on the forward edge, racing to and fro, his tunic off, waving it frantically.

"Fire!" he screamed at the top of his lungs. "The roof top is on fire, there … help!"

He pointed to roofs in the distance.

A weight of silence befell the crowd. The yell of "Fire" terrorized all, and even on the most perfect of days, when nothing seemingly could go wrong, citizens of Fortune's Gateway still kept ears attuned to the possibility their greatest dread had arisen, and demanded their immediate response. Fire, the common enemy of all. Lives and fortunes might be lost in an instant.

Needless to say, all turned to face the call. At first they saw nothing, until their eyes rested on the figure of a young mountain boy, jumping wildly about on the front edge of an adjoining rooftop, any lowland child would surely have already fallen, calling for their attention to fire somewhere to the west, but yet out of their view. Some began running to investigate, others knew to gather containers for water. First to the front were the soldiers of Wei, sent to capture the child, now finally located.

Even those in the circle and witnessing from the stage could not disregard the call. Only one person in the entire arena knew to ignore it, and that person happened not to be the Black Knight.

When Black turned his head ever so slightly, more from curiosity than from concern, the spell on Li weakened. The Black Knight sensed the subtle change in the balance of energy and knew instantly he had fallen prey to nothing more than a clever distraction, a ruse perpetuated by a child nonetheless.

His rage now in clear focus, he turned back toward Li. No more time for games. He exploded forward with the wand in his right hand whipping downward and across in an angled trajectory targeting the left coronal suture, expecting to explode Li Fung's head, drain dry the life within, strike fear into all, and finally slam shut the door on this whole affair.

Li, senses again returned, had seized the diversion to gain position, and superior geometry. Now Red closed from his rear once again, intending to explode toward Li's spine with his feared twisting palm strike. Li stepped right foot forward toward Black into the classical position of single whip, diverting the deadly wand with his left hand in chicken head position, driving his open right hand forward, mounted tightly upon the authority of his cutting thought.

Black had no concern; he knew he had moved first, and was the quicker. Natural laws were natural laws after all. Li had already lost the opportunity for first contact. Li's right hand thrust, targeting the Knight's right chest at shoulder would never make final contact. Li would be dead by then.

But then again, the venerable Black Knight had never before encountered a master of the cutting thought.

From the center of his being, some say a point three finger widths below the naval and two thirds the distance from abdomen to back, Li exploded a seed of energy which, within him, rode atop a wave ascending from the ground coursing through his body, harnessed by his thought and bent by his will, finally funneled through the delicate, but perfect channels of single whip and propelled out the palm of his right hand where it coalesced into an orb of a different sort. Not at all like the sphere atop the mace; nothing shiny, infinitely dark, enticing, or mystifying. Just there, on the underside of vision, a ball of white light, now charging maddeningly ahead like an unbridled and relentless Red Hare[18].

The lightning bolt of impact into Black's closing shoulder could be heard everywhere in the plaza as an unmistakable crack, like the weighted branch of a massive tree snapping suddenly under load from an uncompromising wind.

The alarming sound pulled everyone's attention back to the stage. Some were sure the framing beneath had failed,

---

[18] Guan Gung's famed steed, previously mentioned.

and expected to see it drop to the ground under its own weight. First fire, now this, what next?

Instead, they witnessed Black reeling backwards, his right shoulder and arm contorted grotesquely as though the joints at shoulder, elbow and wrist had lost their connections, and the anatomical elements twisted in ways which pained others just to see. The mace of death flew from his now useless grip; captured mid air by Li's anticipating left hand.

The Match Concludes

Geometry, one would do well to master it. And of course, the thought which cuts, if only someone can be found who can explain it.

Red adjusted to the shifting target before him and poured back into action. Jumping forward, he snaked his lead arm around Li's neck and wrapped him in the feared naked choke, a move which would have been impossible had Li not been so distracted by the orb he now held, and the many voices calling for release from within. The Red Knight knew from long experience to ignore the sphere. For him, the endgame reduced to incapacitating Li by cutting all blood flow to his brain and then getting the hell out of there.

With his size and prodigious strength, Red lifted Li effortlessly from the ground, holding him high and rootless, body weight pulling downward from the neck. Li's vision fogged from the giant's right arm tightening even more and constricting blood vessels and nerves on both sides. As he flayed about, Red's left hand leveraged against his rear skull. Now, he felt his head tipping frighteningly forward,

compressing the trachea into a knot. Li Fung's brain readied
to turn to useless pulp. He couldn't breathe. His ever
trusted focus already gone, Li dangled like a fish on a line
appearing beaten and ineffective. Unable to bear the
inevitable, the crowd turned its eyes away. He fought
within himself to glean what little strength and willpower
remained. Using his right arm to support the left, he
struggled to raise the weighted orb rearward to where he
could bring the ball hard down upon the top of Red's head.
His target, "Bai Hui", the point of a hundred convergences.
Perhaps only a diversion at best, but in the moment, the only
option remaining before quick death.

He struck once, nothing; then a second time, still nothing.
Was he even making contact? Consciousness now seeping
from innate awareness, all his strength drained. Just when
life's vision turned toward shadow did he manage to
somehow strike the third time. It felt to be barely a touch.

A sudden stillness. The red giant, who had been brutally
maneuvering to neutralize his every move, had suddenly
frozen.

Li had nothing left, his appendages hung limp. He
wondered if he were still even holding the mace. He
prepared himself for the brutalization certain to follow.

Then, unexpectedly, he felt his world tilting backwards,
his body still tight in the giant's grip. His mind flashed an
image of a massive tree falling groundward, a panda still
anchored alongside its trunk, helpless to do anything. Then
he crashed with the titan onto the floor of the stage. At
impact, the savage death grip fell lose of its own accord, and

Li rolled from atop his body and ascended to his right, forcing what hold remained to open and release.

He knew first to sight on Yellow, who made no move. Yellow could see Li's face had turned ashen. He recognized the shades of energy, and knew Li, seemingly as agile as ever, was acting on instinct only, as he had nothing left beyond what it took to simply stand there and flash his ever present, seemingly all comprehending smile. A renewed understanding crossed between them. Though no words passed, as originally agreed, Yellow would stand to, and not unleash his attack until Li signaled his readiness.

Just then, a huge hand grabbed Li's left arm from behind and spun him rearward. The Black Knight had come for his Assassin's Mace, without which he would be nothing. Li hop stepped delicately then landed like a light-footed cat squaring on his foe, clasping his hands tightly along the mace's handle. Instinctively, he dropped his left leg rearward into a reverse bow as he angled his forearms over the giant's grip and arced the handle groundward, breaking free from the hold. Needle at sea bottom[19]! Now confronted by the orb, the giant froze.

The scribe stood suddenly from his seat and called out, "Time has run. Stop! The match is over!"

---

[19] One of the classic postures incorporated into the forms of modern Tai Chi. In its many permutations, what remains common is the incorporation of extreme leverage to redirect incoming energy from its intended target, downing it to ground.

Liang San leaped into the circle, judiciously positioning between Li Fung and the two remaining knights.

The Black Knight, still formidable, but naked without his mace, demanded, "Return my weapon!" then glared impatiently to Liang San for assistance.

Only then did Li Fung have opportunity to take in the terrible finality which befell the once intimidating and fearless Red Knight. He stepped back and looked down. There in his magnificent courtly regalia lay what had moments before been a fearsome giant. Now he looked to be no more than a rotted timber, disguised grotesquely as a human, face barely visible in its shriveled bark, mockingly attired as an imperial knight.

Li couldn't help but to crouch down and look hard into the now sealed eyes, wondering if any trace of the once terror rendering life remained within. With his free hand he ran curious fingers over the surface, only to have it powder and collapse inward from the delicate stroke of his touch.

The eyes of Yellow glossed on seeing this. Of the companion knights, only Red had been a true friend.

Outside the circle, Long Hsieh, not fully resigned to defeat, glanced to the western plaza for a sign of his squad and the boy who yelled "fire." There, he saw on the same rooftop, one of his men signaling the child had been found.

"This has not yet played to its final end."

Liang San stared at the mace, still in Master Li's left hand, then looked at the Red giant, and recalled the seeming spell cast over Li in the midst of combat. *"What the hell is that cursed thing?"* For once, albeit without the valued counsel of his man Fa Miu, Liang San knew exactly how to respond.

"There were no weapons permitted in this match, and accordingly, no weapon taken need be returned. You have asked for return of a weapon. What was forbidden in the first, need not be returned in the last!" With a cut of his hand and a firm shake of his head in the direction of the Black Knight he left no doubt as to where he stood.

The Black Knight heard only the loud ringing in his ears, and the voice from deep within bemoaning the loss. He saw the signal from Liang San and knew its meaning.

The Headsman then looked to Li Fung.

Master Li thought only of the mace. As he held it, it spoke to him, reaching for his most base desires, cajoling his ambitions, promising the impossible. He didn't understand the weapon, but stood witness to its power and recognized its unspeakable evil. Even as he stood, he somehow heard whispers from across the circle; the cries of greed, ambition, and cruelty emitting their pleading chorus from the center of where Black stood. *"Am I hallucinating? No, even my own voice calls the same longings to me ..."* As he stood, he could scarcely think, so loud and distracting had become the several competing voices and their cacophony of calls for its soul grabbing power.

He could not say what he would do with it, but of one thing he had become certain. It could not stay with him. He had already been tainted by the ways of the world and knew he could not resist its allure.

He looked across to the Black Knight, raised the wand, and voiced, "If you really want it, come now and see if you can take it from me."

Even in his soundless world, the Black Knight knew what had been said, and that he had been challenged. For the first time in his eventful life, he tasted the fear he had delivered to countless others. Where does the orb take its victims? How can life be made to instantly disappear? For himself, he wanted no part of the answers to these questions, and knew his exalted existence had been forever undone. A taste bitter beyond all imagining.

Only when he replaced its cover and bound it tightly over the orb did Li Fung stop hearing its disturbing calls.

Saving One's Face

Fa Miu marveled at the child's ploy. In his own mind he had run reality's scales of presumed outcomes, frozen in their moment of delicate balance, suddenly tipped to one side by the least expected of all things. The sudden weight of a straw dog placed high on the altar of notice. In the end, the ruse had turned the outcome.

"Hui, what made you think to yell 'Fire'?"

"Would something else have worked better?" asked the boy, somewhat puzzled.

"No, young man, it was perfect for the moment, and your timing can only be described as exquisite. But did Li know you would be doing this?"

"Maybe."

"Maybe?"

"Yes, he told me I would be his eyes from the rear. He warned me of tricks, and assassins. When I asked how I should give warning ..."

"Of course, he **told** you to yell 'Fire!' "

"I thought he was joking when he said it. I didn't pay it much mind. Luckily I remembered it when I did."

Fa Miu smiled, then looked intently to Shi-Hui Ke, recalling how he had been told to remember the boy's name, "It seems with Li Fung, nothing happens quite by accident. Tell me young man, what did you make of his cutting thought?"

Hui had to think on this a bit. *"Was the call of fire also part of Master Li's cutting thought?"* But before he could answer, a number of loud voices ordered them not to move. Fa Miu put the boy behind him as the squad from Wei came at them from multiple directions on the rooftop.

Fa Miu gestured openly with his hands, directing his attention to the presumed squad leader, "How may we help you."

The officer recognized Fa Miu as the town adjutant. "We've come for the boy, sir. He interfered with the competition, we need to bring him below and establish his relationship to Li Fung. The outcome will likely be disputed. It need not concern you."

His willingness to keep Fa Miu out of the mix was meant as courtesy.

"Ah, then I must acknowledge your remarkable skill in anticipating events about to happen. Before any of this, you were searching for the child down below. Don't waste our time with denials. I already know you interrogated the shop keepers. Interference with the competition? You were sniffing his trail long before any call of 'Fire!' and what followed.

"You know you have no authority to act independently in this jurisdiction, particularly when you haven't elicited our consent or cooperation. And that's what you're doing right now. Your curious movements through the crowd drew my attention, and I deemed it prudent to investigate, if only to assist in quelling a problem. The 'problem' turned out to be the boy, and your questions to the shopkeepers as to his whereabouts further piqued my curiosity. I asked myself, 'What possible interest could the guests from Wei have in a boy from the mountain tribes?' Kind fate deemed it best I find him first. Now, I am left with only questions, but as of yet, no answers. Being adjutant, I will unravel this. That's what I do around here. As it stands, I am assuming full responsibility for the child, until we can clear the matter. Perhaps it can be easily reconciled. If you will, Captain, explain to me. Who sent you for the boy, and for what reason would you or they have any interest in a child such as this? It makes no sense, and troubles me, a humble servant who wishes only harmony and simplicity. Please, don't give me a load of horseshit. My courtesy and patience thin quickly."

The squad leader of course could reveal nothing of his orders, or from whence they came. Nor could he leave without the child. To admit acting under Long Hsieh's directive would be tantamount to admission of deceit and treachery, an irreversible loss of face for the Wei Minister.

Though having been humiliated by events below, Long Hsieh could still, albeit in faux graciousness, concede defeat while acknowledging the match had been fairly played (for the most part). In his concession he would be sure to stress that Li Fung, clearly a "planted master of the highest caliber and skill" had made his point against champions of Wei, who on this day, had all but won but for the unfortunate distraction of a child's yelling fire, when in fact there was none. A questionable serendipity at best.

It would have been enough to save, even regain some degree of face.

You see, the Westerners understood courtesy, and valued graciousness when winning, or losing. It had long been their feeling that playing the game and living the special moment far outvalued the rewards or the consequences, and they expected this to be freely acknowledged by both the victor and the fallen in the aftermath. Failing in this represented a serious breach of courtesy, and loss of face likely long remembered.

Liang San, as a point of generosity, had allowed Long Hsieh time to do just that, but Long Hsieh stood, fuming and glaring at the two knights yet standing. Under any other circumstances, he would have ordered Li Fung's death, and for added good measure, the death of Liang San, as fair retribution for his perceived duplicity in the outrage. The frontmost crowd read all of this in the harsh angles and contortions so evident in his expression. Their whispers of concern over what they saw rippled quickly from front to rear.

"Give the minister fair chance to concede," retorted some in the crowd.

So, they waited.

For Long Hsieh, yet anticipating the boy's imminent capture, he saw only this single residual play. He would trade the boy for the mace and the Black Knight would have his demon stick once again. With that returned, he could then settle up with Li Fung, perhaps the boy too. The outcome would then be formally protested, and eventually turned. Their petrified corpses would grace road posts along the north exit from Fortune's Gateway footing their native hills as warning to others like them.

"The message would be unmistakable, they may not like us, but they will know we mean business, and will have our way before all others." thought Long Hsieh. Those in the Wei court would surely approve.

Fa Miu - "The Fox"

A Fox Is a Fox Is a Fox!

Fa Miu continued, "I understand if you can't answer, Captain. If that's the case, I have no option but to beg your leave, and place the boy in the charge of Li Fung for proper return to his people."

"We can not allow that sir!"

"How so? Under what authority do you make demands on me? Can you name anyone better suited to see to the boy's well being than his own tribesman? One who has already proven himself to be beyond capable?"

The Captain of the guard stood there, for the moment frozen, now pasted cleverly into a little corner. Anything he did or said left him no better than where he stood, and where he stood led to disappointment and disgrace. That clever fox Fa Miu had put him here. Desperate for a way out, his mind raced and tumbled through everything that had occurred up until that point, then settled inexplicably on Fa Miu's comment "Your movements through the crowd came to my attention, and I deemed it prudent to investigate."

"Son of a bitch! No one even knows he's up here!"

Only then did he see his solution. *"I can be clever too, even a sly fox like Fa Miu can drift too far from his den."* He signaled to his men, "Kill Fa Miu! Take the boy!"

Why does it always boil down to violence? I suppose it could have worked. The body of town adjutant Fa Miu found inexplicably murdered on a rooftop, the boy, bound, gagged and hauled off like a piglet in a sack. Displayed before all as the prime suspect, and now known to be acting in complicity with Li Fung. Why, this kept getting better the more one went with it.

The thoughts ran away with his focus, *"An accomplishment like this would bring me notice even within the imperial court. From there, no telling where it might lead."*

But for one miscalculation. A failure to register completely what lay immediately before his eyes.

No sooner had the Captain given his orders, than he lay dead. A single strike from the practiced hand of Fa Miu.

We should know not to "Count our chickens before they ... "

Little Hui had heard of the iron death hand, just as he had heard of the cutting thought, but until this day, had questioned whether either existed in fact as opposed to wish or imagination[20]. He had only moments before witnessed Li's defeat of the Black Knight, set up by a devastating blow dealt without so much as a discernible touch. Now, having to take in this new feat, young Hui allowed how Fa Miu's iron death hand represented a miracle with a different pedigree, but of proportionate import.

The "fox" had been standing no more than a forearm's distance from the chest of the squad leader. No sooner had the loathsome order been given, than Fa Miu exploded into motion, his left foot springing forward, his right foot lifting, then dropping back and anchoring, a supporting piston for his right arm which shot ahead and outward like a festival rocket, compressing the once Captain's chest into a full inversion. Realizing Fa Miu's hand couldn't even be seen, so deeply had it embedded into their leader, the remaining four stood motionless, momentarily gripped by awe. Silently, they weighed possible fall back options in lieu of this, yet another unanticipated ripple in what started out a simple task.

How much easier do our machinations play, when what we expect can be counted on to occur as we expect it to. True indeed, but alas, not for them on this particular day.

To a person, their mental gyrations concluded nearly the same. They could not afford to return empty handed, let

------

[20] Back in the ice shelter, Bao Ling, now listening even more intently to Hui's tale wondered if his old mentor, Iron Hand Gao had somehow figured into this. What Fa Miu reportedly did certainly raised the question. He must remember to ask Hui.

alone without their leader, and still justify their continued existence. So, even though they portioned a degree of serious thought to running for their own skins, they knew they were in the stew either way. At least if they came back with the child, there might be hope of a reward, certainly redemption, possibly even a promotion, doubly so if one of them might further distinguish himself by taking out Fa Miu.

Oh … right … Fa Miu. Who would have reckoned his kung fu to be so strong? A problem there. Regardless, too late now for such concerns or considerations. They were soldiers weren't they? Warriors. Tried and battle proven, time and again.

Once your foot gets enmeshed in a trap, wondering how you got there and why you weren't elsewhere makes no difference in your dilemma. Life can sometimes be like that. Seemingly stuck in a never ending cascade of predicaments, ever hoping all will somehow fall into place. Just get by this one irksome problem, and move on. For these soldiers, and others like them, the eternal quandary.

It shouldn't surprise if our remaining four squad members had differing takes on what to do. The younger and more enterprising two had no mind to wait for the others. The two grizzled elders seemed timid and to have no heart in acting, at least not yet.

They might have followed the example of their elders, or listened to their better minds before launching toward Fa Miu. To Shi-Hui Ke's measuring eyes, they appeared to be moving indecisively, a bit too cautiously. Not one to idle carelessly, Fa Miu knew to strike when the opportunity presented. Just be certain the opportunity wasn't cast as bait. By their movements and their inclinations, each seeming to defer initiative to the other, the two unwittingly opened themselves to the "swarming bees" counter. He capitalized on their stutters and stalls with five incapacitating strikes for every one of their wild and undisciplined sweeping arcs, all the while making sure in his peripheral scan, the others remained where they stood.

Young Hui had never seen the likes of it, even from Master Li, whom the child figured knew everything there was to know. The strategy relied on quick and decisive strikes, from all directions and angles, as unpredictable and overwhelming as an angry swarm of bees, hence its appearance, and its name.

But far more lay beneath the surface of what the child witnessed. By cutting back on the power of the strikes, the defender Fa Miu placed them with greater speed, care and precision, unerringly targeting a nerve plexus, blood channel, or meridian with each impact. That's how it is. Power, speed, precision, you can really only possess two in any given instant. Sensitive points have their quirks and peculiarities. The same point struck several times in quick succession weakens, and ignites, sometimes with incapacitating pain, sometimes with less expected discomforts (nausea perhaps, or other more embarrassing discharges). Combinations of points can work together, their inclinations combining into dark symphonies. Once encouraged, toxic energies leapfrog one over the other, triggered by impacts measuring little more than glancing touches. On release, they rush like deadly venoms to some intended endpoint deep within the opponent. It might be the spleen, could be the liver or the kidney, perhaps the heart or even the triple warmer, and others akin. Places sometimes not even there as true organs, but defined by traditional concepts of function and flows of energy. Great minds, over endless spans of time, took meticulous care in mapping these organs defined by function, and their propensities, basing their studies and conclusions on endless experimentations, and meticulous accountings of outcomes. The end result, a science of metaphor, where symbols and words defined otherwise functional but seemingly disconnected realities. Though inexplicable, they stood on their own philosophical underpinnings with the strength of observed fact and documented outcome. You see, one equipped with proper knowledge and awareness regarding the subtleties of sequencing holds great advantage over an illness, or disease, or even an opponent. This particular fighting science had evolved as half sister to the profound breakthroughs in traditional medicine up until that point. The fighting science had nothing to do with healing, it represented the reverse, though it relied on and stemmed from the same fundamental roots. Some were quite adept at both. It's always like that, isn't it? Something with great promise for good sooner or later sprouts a sinister twin. The dark science of point attacks relied for its malignancy on the very art of healing. Fortunately, few had mastered its secrets and as of yet, the practice had not fully bridged into darkness. It had been gifted to Fa Miu by his own teacher, but only after decades of tutelage and observation, and ultimately full trust in Fa Miu's impeccable character. Besides, of all the students the teacher had ever mentored, only Fa Miu had the requisite underlying skills to fully take command of, and to engage the art. More often than not, it backfired on those less capable.

The effects? One possessing such skills could pause respiration, or the function of a spleen or liver, or even in the most dire of circumstances, stop the heart. Most don't believe these things are even possible, or argue the effects of these strategies vary unpredictably with the times of day, flow of the seasons or transits of the moon, making them impossible to harness or to govern. They might justify themselves pointing out the obvious, "Even if it were all true, what person in the middle of combat might be so adept as to be able to execute at will a combination of contacts, strikes and touches, all carefully mapped to produce an intended effect within a precisely determined slice of time, without first getting his block knocked off by an opponent. Why, even one such as Guan Gung himself, supreme in the arts, has not been said or rumored to have been given over to such foolishness."

Hearing the likes of that, Colonel Sun[21] would have strenuously objected.

The "Poisoned Hand." That's what the techniques were called in later times. Eventually kept close hold within the walls of Shaolin, they were rarely ever seen again.

---

[21] Colonel Sun. Contemporary of Lord Guan, and one who would certainly have known. The two friends often shared their many secrets as they tested skills one against the other.

So most, like these two young guards, never gave much thought or concern to it, figuring they would never encounter anyone so gifted as to be able to pull it off.

To be explicitly fair, we don't know what Fa Miu did in fact. In any instance, it would have taken very special men to survive the blows he delivered. To Shi-Hui Ke, it seemed almost to be an illusion, he even had to blink and look twice. Fa Miu became a visual blur so fluid and gifted as to be moving freely about while the two attackers stood leadfooted. Their rival, now nemesis selected strike points with utmost care, delivering his own recipe of sequenced contacts and impacts with intended outcomes we can only speculate upon.

The two fell dead where they stood.

Get the Boy!

Can't say it surprised the boy. By this point, he was getting used to it.

Now noting the others cycling threateningly about, Hui wondered if he should be helping, but on seeing Fa Miu's frequent concerned glances his way, making certain he remained safe and out of harm's way, Hui decided it best to hold ground and not complicate things.

"I will watch his blind side, warn him if necessary, just like with Master Li" And with that, he kept close eye on the remaining two. *"Still, it's best to be prepared."* He reached stealthily into his pouch and pulled out a small patch of goatskin around which were wrapped two long strands of carefully braided hemp cord. These devices were common tools for men of the hills, even those as young as Hui, always having to protect their animals from predators. He fished even more deeply to the bottom of the pouch where he knew he would find three very special friends. Little treasures of a war-child, defined not by wealth or inheritance, but by little more than pride, integrity, and an emerging self awareness.

His treasures were stones, nearly perfectly rounded and still in their natural state. Of the thousands he had screened while traversing the high country, these three stood most perfect above all. They were beautiful, and flawless, their weight, density and balance evidenced by the clear high pitched click when one tapped another. Then there was the true and even roll when he took any which one to a table and simply pushed it, admiring its unerringly straight run, with no drift or uncertainty of purpose whatsoever. One appeared to be a piece of petrified wood, with a bit of a cat's eye, at times seemingly alive. He often stared at it under the sun, and then the moon, trying to understand what it saw from within. Another a rosy quartz, when in one's hand, almost like peering at a spherical flower held in timeless suspension. The third, gray, like a water laden cloud, some type of metal judging by its weight, much heavier than its counterparts. Toughest of the three, he had used it many times in the past to hunt, and it had survived his occasional miscues without blemish, no less for the wear.

He put all three into his left hand, being sure to hold the gray ball in readiness between thumb and forefinger. As always, it would be his first choice. He then unwound the cords from the goatskin wrap, keeping close eye on the sentries and Fa Miu. One cord he anchored with its slip loop to his right middle finger, the other he held tightly between his right thumb and the side of his forefinger, using a marker knot along the cord to ensure both lengths were precisely the same measure once in readiness. He looked down to the goatskin, now nearly touching his ankle, then lifted the sling to load the gray ball into its center. Once placed, he let the apparatus hang limply by his side, for when and if needed.

Two of the sentries remained, the most seasoned of the original five. They had tasted combat many times and were not timid. Pure, unadulterated professional soldiers. For them, this was just another job. They had families; once; and children; and parents. Even now their guilt laden thoughts reminded them incessantly of failed intentions of sending money and maybe even captured gold to those needing their support at home. Money, gold, none ever seemed to land their way or to cross their palms. So without the means or ability to support their families and loved ones they did only what they knew to do ... keep on keeping[22] on, with their interminable self reproach always at hand to give them company. Like most everyone in these type binds, they long ago lost track of what they once cherished most, and with that, what they started out hoping to become. All which remained lay before them, subject to their instinct for self preservation.

So you see, on this day, killing for them would come easy.

Though not necessarily friends, they often depended one on the other to ensure mutual survival. In their world, alone almost certainly meant death. You were far better off if you had a trusty always at your back. Their mutual skills had been honed razor sharp over years together and endless encounters jointly survived. Even before they set out on their current mission, they knew from long experience their Captain was marked to be a certain goner. If not this day,

---

[22] Said no where better than in the lyrics to Bob Dylan's *Tangled Up in Blue.*

then another close on its tail. Never, ever expose your vitals to anyone, particularly when you meant to do them ill. He had made a habit of it, and today, had finally paid the band for his dancing with idiocy.

Their two younger and more ambitious counterparts? Fools, just like countless others before them. Driven to lunacy by fear, compounded by reckless, even careless timing. All propelled by pointless and ill-considered ambition. Even their final attack, which could have been their shining moment, lacked heart and true commitment. Never, ever attack if you're not prepared to risk all in the moment.

Having yet again confirmed the boy to be safe, Fa Miu cautiously stared their way. *"These two will be a problem,"* thought Fa Miu. He saw earlier how they waited wisely rather than entering the fray with the others, whose ineptitude and inexperience would only have gotten in their more polished way. Now that the dead weight had been cleared, the job, as it had so often before, fell to them.

Fa Miu shifted right hoping to gain angle on one and avoid the other. Without even thinking, they adjusted instinctively, keeping Fa Miu as third point on their tactical triangle, then together, began to trim the length of their respective sides.

Now, they maneuvered to close upon him for the kill. Like skilled hunters stalking a wolf and cub, they kept their prey centered, then cautiously turned the geometry to force Fa Miu to where he could no longer protect the boy.

"Just a bit more" thought the senior of the two. *"We will have the boy; and you will meet the justice of Wei when we report your killing of the Captain and the two squadsmen. With a careful bit of polish, no one will doubt how your sympathy for the renegade mountain people drew you into a plot to steal the match for Li Fung. The day will yet belong to Wei, as will Fortune's Gateway."*

Shi-Hui Ke stood motionless, noting Fa Miu's quick glance, his heightened concern not lost on the boy. The fox now realized the child had become vulnerable to capture by the rightmost sentry. Once in hand, the other would cover while his partner went below with the child and called for reinforcements.

Having no choice Fa Miu angled to initiate attack against the greater threat, putting the boy's safety above all other concerns. He had to drive that opponent back, and away from the child. The sentry's senior partner stood in the ready anticipating this very prospect and moved from behind to close the trap. Hoping to protect his rear, Fa Miu sprung to the air opening the distance behind. The sentry to his front had readied for this. It had in fact, been the only option available to Fa Miu, and though he executed it beautifully, a straightaway forward kick with his right leg, and a spinning wheel kick with his left, neither found its mark. No matter. Fa Miu first needed distance from the rear sentry, and while airborne had readied his hands for a killing barrage on the lead guard once landed. Instead, he met with the sentry's perfectly executed Kau, a bump with the shoulder which drilled through the center of his midline, long taught as one of the ancient "old reliables."[23] A well executed Kau could kill instantly. Few possessed such skill. This sentry came close. Met squarely by his adversary's right shoulder, perfectly rooted over a right foot placed forward into side dragon stance; Fa Miu felt like he had run full speed into the pointed corner of a fortress wall.

Nearly senseless, he bounced, staggered, then fell back, legs crumbling beneath as he landed limply on the ground.

Like a panther, the senior closed his distance from the rear, now pulling loose his killing blade, ordering his partner, "Get the boy, I'll take care of ..."

---

[23] It is said the legendary swordsman, Miyamoto Mushashi had also mastered this strike, and engaged it effectively in a number of his contests.

Honor Sinks Its Teeth

He would have finished his sentence with "him!" but just as the word touched the tip of his tongue the sun went dark, and all sound lifted from the air about him.

For what seemed no small eternity, he floated on a cloud of nothing, seeing nothing, hearing nothing, and even eventually, knowing nothing. Then it all stopped. Compared to most, and considering the possibilities, and what he otherwise might have deserved from a karmic perspective, it had been a good and peaceful parting for him, though quite abrupt and unexpected.

Just moments before, from where he lay inauspiciously exposed on the rooftop, ignoring his own dour predicament Fa Miu's attention never left Shi-Hui Ke, now almost certain to be captured. The fox's thoughts groped for a last tactic to foil the effort, but wait, *"What's the boy doing? What's that in his hands?"*

He saw young Hui with sling now in full view circling once by his right side, then lifting in an accelerating whip like circle over his head. He released just as he stepped forward with his left leg, providing balance and perfect root. The now turned loose trigger cord snapped forward with a loud crack like the tongue of an angry dragon. The sentry turning toward Shi-Hui Ke nearly stumbled when he saw his partner drop like a sack of rice, motionless, a pool of blood and gray matter pouring from the side of his opened skull. The man stood agape, at first having no clue what happened, then from the corner of his eye caught a small gray sphere rolling slowly away and catching stillness between roof tiles.

"You little bastard! A sling, of all things!" he mumbled, perhaps to himself. "No time for this!!!" Then with renewed determination he charged toward the boy.

By then, the boy had recovered the flailing cord. But without time to reload, he could only snap the trigger end forward, like a whip, knowing from Master Li's training to direct the marker knot toward the eyes of his assailant.

It purchased a sparing moment, nothing more.

Shi-Hui Ke knew he had to move quickly. Wasting no time or motion, he caught the released cord and reset the knot between his thumb and forefinger, in the same sweep he slid his left hand downward and set his cat's eye carefully into the center of the cradle.

Fa Miu may still have been dazed but when he saw the remaining sentry dash for the boy he instinctively reached for the blade from the downed partner, then pushed fully to his feet just as the sentry closed on Shi-Hui Ke, who had already begun to wind his second shot.

The sentry moved too quickly for the boy's release. Before the projectile took flight, the sentry had the child by the throat, lifting him from the ground and pinning him to the parapet, where in an instant, he struck and knocked the child senseless. Without even removing it from the boy's hand, he grabbed for the sling, coiled the cord tightly around the child's neck then threw him face down to the tiles where with the free end, he cuffed Hui's arms behind his back and knotted them firm. Even a full grown man could not have pulled free from this deadly hog tie without first choking himself.

Not unexpectedly, he heard a movement from his side, and knew it could only be Fa Miu. He had wanted to finish Fa Miu when he went down, maybe he should have, but first things first. The boy had to be immobilized, or all would be lost. He had no other options, his partner now gone. Finally, the boy lay secure, and as Fa Miu approached, *"I have to give it to the adjutant, the guy has balls!"* the last sentry stood and faced the fox. He still held the cord, and with his hard tug, compressed the loop even more tightly on the boy's neck, now a deep purple. Fa Miu saw the child go limp, all awareness of his surrounds gone.

"So, it all comes to this Mr. Town Adjutant. What do you propose we do from here?"

In the art of warfare, this represented an invitation to parlay, and was not lost on Fa Miu.

The sentry had only this single play. Assuming Fa Miu to be like every other rising and ambitious man he had ever encountered, he figured the adjutant would instantly recognize the advantage of an alliance, the two of them bringing the boy down, and letting the devils below work out the details, covers, and explanations, while they basked in Wei's rewards.

Fa Miu stood before him, perfectly relaxed, right shoulder slightly back from left, his right arm hanging down, the gripped blade concealed in the folds of his robe.

"I told you earlier, the boy stands under my protection. I asked you not give me a load of horseshit. You and your friends did just that. Surely, by now you've learned I am not a patient man. I ask you once again. Please step aside and allow us to pass."

With those words, he stopped and waited for some reaction or acknowledgment from the sentry, still clinging to the leash securing Hui's arms and throat, and further cutting blood flow to his head. Fa Miu had hoped the sentry would let it go, and run for his life. With him gone, it would have made explanations and accountings much simpler in the aftermath. Besides, another death now just seemed pointless.

A matter of perspectives perhaps. For the soldier, death did not present the worst of possible outcomes. What opportunity lay in this moment was all he had after a lifetime of disappointments and unfilled aspirations. Losing again here, and living as he had before would be far more troubling than the prospect of death. No way was he giving up now. The boy had become his ticket, death paled in comparison to this opportunity.

Fa Miu saw this, and he saw the boy at death's door. With deep regret he whipped the knife forward and out, slashing the sentry's throat, killing him in cold blood.

He had no intention of experiencing Kao a second time.

So much for honor.

He had sworn to protect the boy. As though speaking to the lords of his own conscience, he whispered, *"Let honor sink its teeth into that!"*

"A sling, of all things!"

A Gang of Thugs

From the stage below, Long Hsieh feared something had yet again gone wrong.

While everyone in the plaza focused on the stage and hoped for the Minister to break silence and affirm the results, Long Hsieh studied the rooftops and saw the child standing motionless, only now facing the other direction.

What could possibly be going on? Why haven't they brought him down?

In that moment, even Li Fung stared, equally puzzled.

Suddenly, the silhouette of a Wei sentry appeared to seize the boy, pulling him from view.

Seeing this, Long Hsieh had good reason to believe his fortunes had finally turned. He took a deep confident breath, then turned slowly to stage center, yet said nothing. *"How best to play this?"* He nodded guilefully to Li Fung, already plotting his ultimate unraveling and end soon to follow.

Li Fung could only acknowledge the nod, *"What in hell does he have up his sleeve now?"*

Not having a clue as to the back game being played, town headsman Liang San prayed for the quick re-emergence of his adjutant. Fa Miu would certainly know how to smooth all of this over.

Tense moments passed. No one moved or spoke.

On the rooftop, Fa Miu quickly untied the child, slapping him once across the face, "Hui, come to! It's over. We must leave. Wake up boy!"

Quick enough, his eyes opened wide. There in Fa Miu's hands, a blooded knife. At the boy's feet, the man who had struck him, now looking to have two mouths, the small one pursed tightly in determination, the second, below, its dripping red lips grinning wildly as though having one final laugh over the madness of it all.

"Can you walk on your own?"

A quick nod of affirmation as the boy jumped to his feet. With relief, he reached for his sling and found the cat's eye still there.

Fa Miu grabbed his hand, guiding him alongside the ridge parapet to an opening below the crown gable. Suddenly the boy pulled loose.

"Hui, get back here!"

Like a small cat, the boy backtracked then dropped flat to the surface, scanning the overlapping tiles until at last he found what he had been looking for.

"My missing treasure!"

He hurriedly picked it up, ran back to Fa Miu, then held it for him to see. A perfectly rounded gray ball.

"Ah, indeed, a treasure; one which has proven its worth and should be honored accordingly!"

"His friends missed him sir, and pleaded I go back to find him," answered the child, now holding up all three for Fa Miu's scrutiny.

"Yes, keep them close to you always little one, and you will be safe with the very heart of your homeland sitting in your pouch. Enough now, come!"

The boy gave his hand again to the man, and in a moment they were off the roof. Inside, they found their way to the central hall where they met what at first appeared to be a gang of thugs ascending the stairwell, toting sticks and clubs, some even waving bronze jians[24].

The boy already pulled loose and started to reach for his sling when the lead man called, "Adjutant Fa, we were

---

[24] Two edged swords.

worried. The Wei troopers were looking for the child, then you came. We grew concerned when they turned about and followed your path into here; we suspected trouble and knew something was up. Who do they think they are, guests, acting like they own the town. I rounded up some muscle to even the tally just in case. Let them see who they can push around now!"

Adjutant Fa stepped forward, clearly touched his townspeople would think to assume such risks on his behalf, eyes welling with tears of gratitude. He didn't know what to say, or what to reveal.

He opted to play it straight with them.

"Boys, I've got a big problem."

"What, Sir? We're with you. Tell us what you need us to do!"

"I'm worried about getting you involved ..."

"Nonsense! We're with you and the boy, rice in the pot, all in the heat together!"

"I must tell you, the squad from Wei is still out there." He nodded toward the opening beneath the crown gable, leading to the roof.

The lead man furled his brow, then signaled for one of his fellows to discreetly peer through the portico to the roof. The man hastened back and whispered his findings to the boss, who instantly dropped to one knee holding the hand over fist salute high over his head toward Fa Miu.

"Sir, have no concerns, we're in with you, all the way!"

Fa Miu stepped to the leader, took his hands and respectfully lifted him to standing. "They must be discretely removed from the roof and all traces and evidence eradicated. There's little time to do it, but nothing can be left. Not a trace. All of our lives are on the line. Even now, we may be too late, and at risk of getting caught."

"We know what to do sir!"

"The pig farms?" Fa Miu's thoughts raced to the injured simpleton, so unceremoniously and recklessly thrown from the stage earlier that day. For the pig herders, a token of payback. It would not be lost on them. They were a practical and appreciative lot.

The boss nodded, adding, "We'll make sure everything on them disappears as well."

"Remember, all must be destroyed, nothing can be re-sold or preserved, it must appear they simply deserted and left without a trace!"

"Of course sir, we understand completely."

Somehow, Fa Mui knew this was not their first time down this path. He nodded his acceptance and gratitude, adding, "And never a word of this to anyone, ever! A slip of the tongue may well mean our lives!"

The boss man nodded, "Goes without saying sir, you can count on us."

"I am in your debt lads." Fa Miu reached for his purse, emptied it into his right hand, then held it out for the boys to see. Three gold sovereigns, and then some. He passed it to the leader. For him and the gang, not a fortune, but quite enough, even split among them. You could see the joy light in their eyes.

"One question sir, if I may ask?"

"Certainly."

"Who took out the five?"

Fa Miu hesitated, then knowing there could be no further secrets between conspirators such as they had become, answered, "I took out four of them, but got myself into a real fix. If not for the boy, I wouldn't be here."

Eying the sling in the child's hand, the gang leader knew the meaning instantly. He smiled broadly toward Shi-Hui Ke, issued yet another martial bow in salute, this time at the boy and called, "To the Shu warriors, fearless in the face of adversity. May they prosper ten thousand years!"

Shi-Hui Ke reciprocated, proud tears welling in his eyes. He knew of the Shu warriors, and their history and their record of valor. For his name to even be whispered in the same breath carrying the thought of them …

In that instant he knew he had become a man.

The boss turned to Fa Miu, "Be gone sir, we'll have it cleared before you and the lad return to the events below.

And so they did.

Loose Ends

Long Hsieh did not ever get the boy, and the Black Knight never again saw the Assassin's Mace. Without the mace, and his hearing gone; he could no longer fend off the young and ambitious sorts, eager to push their way through him into the elite echelons. In less than the transit of a single season, he fell far and quick in the ranks of Wei, often having to bear ridicule for his failure at Fortune's Gateway; and for his handicap. His hearing gone, along with the loss of his insidious wand, left him at a distinct disadvantage in both combat and challenges, the latter of which had become all too frequent. In the end, for his own survival, he left the troop and took to wandering as a mendicant, begging his way from shrine to shrine. Most knew of his past, and viewed him as evil, steering clear whenever they could. Whatever road he took, he saw no one. When he entered villages and towns, streets emptied and all doors were locked. A goodly number had waited just for this moment to get their just retribution for past wrongs. He remained alone until the end, when one day he disappeared, and was eternally forgotten.

Back in the ring, Long Hsieh stalled a seeming eternity, expecting the child to be produced at any instant and the game finally played to what he deemed its proper climax. Those who went racing to the call of fire returned and made their report to Liang San, among them were the boss and some of his crew. They reported having scoured all the roofs to the west, finding nothing except an inordinate amount of smoke from a drunken back alley pig roast. A false alarm, now confirmed to everyone's relief. Whatever happened between the guards and the child might only be speculated. Long Hsieh could delay no further. The spectators had waited long enough for a concession and clearly their patience had stretched thin. He could say nothing to stall further, nor could he signal concern. Having no other final play, and with a taste infinitely bitter swirling in his mouth, he walked slowly to Li Fung and issued a bow of final acquiescence. He was after all, a skilled politician, and knew well when to salvage what he could.

It proved adequate to the townspeople, who erupted in congratulations for Li Fung's victory, now affirmed. Already the few players who had wagered the long shot, ran about looking to collect their winnings.

As to the squad dispatched to this all important task? Inexplicably, they never returned, nor was any trace of them ever found. At the urging of Minister Long Hsieh himself, Liang San assigned his adjutant Fa Miu to personally oversee the investigation into five missing Wei corpsmen.

Fa Miu skillfully coordinated the combined efforts of the remaining Wei guard with his own constabulary and scoured carefully for days. They found only a handful of witnesses who knew anything, little pieces here and there, but even their recollections were inconsistent and questionable. Several pig farmers from the outskirts of town reported seeing a squad of troopers, numbering maybe four, perhaps seven leaving town, suspiciously traveling off road, appearing to be heading west. They had no other contact with them, and were uncertain even of their uniforms, not knowing how to distinguish the colors of Wei from those of their own constabulary. Fa Miu apologized to his Wei counterparts on their behalf, explaining how it was good they had their pigs, for, given their crude simplicity and ignorance, they would only be victimized by the real world.

His final report, formally presented to Long Hsieh, concluded on the basis of best available evidence the five had deserted and taken to the western wilderness. His Wei counterpart in the investigation concurred fully.

Long Hsieh knew how things might be spun about at court, and how slippery his own status stood relative to the treachery of opportunists in the wings. On his return to the capital, he said nothing of the call of "Fire!" or of his dispatch of a squad to apprehend the boy. *"Why kick sleeping dragons?"* he thought.

What they heard in Wei were tales of a great mountain warrior, who had bested their best. In the years following, Long Hsieh acted dutifully when he counseled the court, "Shu is a quagmire best circumvented or left alone; or in the alternative, treated as a fierce and impregnable state to be courted as an ally. They should never be deemed weak and vulnerable, or cast as an enemy." In that, he upheld his end of the bargain made with Li Fung, who, before all, had bested the Wei Knights.

No one cared to mind that nonsense of course. Those surrounding the Emperor felt Long Hsieh had gone daft. Just another batch looking to push past him to the top. It caused him no worry. He was long experienced in his special craft and knew full well how to sheer the sheep.

No sooner had Fa Miu and the boy made their way to the street than Fa Miu detoured to a back alley tea house where, at his request, the matron of his long acquaintance agreed to mind the child while Fa Miu attended to some urgent business. At the adjutant's request, she loaned some of her own children's clothing, exchanging for the boy's Shu regalia, then had the child join her own in serving the customers. He blended perfectly.

Fa Miu returned to the platform just as Long Hsieh conceded defeat, though still staring with interest toward the western roofs and seeing nothing.

Li Fung graciously thanked the minister for the kind opportunity to make his point, and added his hope more such exchanges might add to a higher mutual understanding and basis for respect in the future.

Take that however you will.

Liang San held tightly to the arm of his trusty Fa Miu, "Where the hell were you? You left me courting disaster here!"

The aid smiled in acknowledgment, "Other issues, very much related to your own, demanded my attention. We will speak over wine, and I will tell you all, then we will laugh heartily over the certain disaster somehow avoided."

And they did.

After the congratulatory rounds concluded, and the crowd started to thin, it was none other than Long Hsieh who suggested Fa Miu escort Li Fung from town, at the least ensuring there would be no hint of scandal or recriminations against Wei and the minister, should anything untoward happen to the tribesman.

To that agreed end, Liang San discretely dispatched eight constables to provide full guard, unseen, but taking the form of a protective shell around the two as they departed town center.

Not until they were under way did Li Fung say, "I must find the boy before leaving. This guard makes that quite difficult, don't you think?"

"I suggest we stop for some tea and refreshments. Was it not your suggestion we share tea once you finished with the honorable Wei delegates."

"My deep regrets" responded a now visibly peeved Li Fung, "Finding the child comes before tea!"

"At this point in time, considering all that has passed, I don't think you will quickly find the boy. Best perhaps to be patient. Maybe you should let the boy find you. Come, let's make a plan together, and have our tea."

Fa Miu's words made sense. For all Li knew, the Wei cadre might still have it in for him, perhaps even trailing their movements at this very instant.

So, tea it was. They sat and spoke of nothing while Li Fung grew all the more tense and impatient. Only when the time came to refill their cups did Li uncover the sly Fox's game. There stood the boy, attired as a local, pouring their tea almost indistinguishable from any of the other staff. Li Fung had to look twice to be sure of his eyes, then rose jubilantly to his feet.

Li and the boy simply stood facing one another, smiling for being together again. Mountain folk were not given to emotional displays. For them, standing still and staring into one another's eyes represented a communion beyond even the answer of prayers.

Li spoke first, "Hui … when you called 'Fire' I was one heartbeat away from my end. The timing could not have been more perfect. What made you choose that moment?"

The boy could only shrug his shoulders, as both men grinned admiringly. Things like this, though accidental to all appearances, never happened independently of a confident, guiding thought. The Fox, and the Master understood this completely. All reduces to timing; a gift possessed by so few. To their eyes, the child's gift spoke for itself.

Young Hui then addressed Li, pointing with his chin (as was their way) toward Fa Miu as he did so, "The Wei sent five soldiers to kidnap me. This man intervened."

"Five soldiers?" puzzled Li Fung, "How did you manage to avoid capture?" He then looked to Fa Miu, expecting to hear of some sort of arrangement or accommodation, perhaps calling even yet for his own approval or complicity.

But Fa Miu said nothing, his eyes told all.

Weighing the gravity of Fox's silence, Li Fung saw as his thoughts raced through various scenarios there could only be one explanation for the child now standing in his presence.

"Hmh! Five ... it appears you've bested me Fa Miu. It took all I could muster to barely survive four (By this point, he considered the Yellow Knight to be a friend). And barely survive I did!"

"You're too polite Master Li. What I did merely echoed your achievement. Like you, I too would not have ended well, had not the boy saved my ass."

Li looked to Shi-Hui Ke, hoping to hear a proud replay of all the details, but Hui, as did the others, had sworn to silence. That did not however interfere with his right hand scribing a barely perceptible circle along his side, possibly replaying in his own mind his kinship with the sling.

"Ah, your sling," said Li Fung.

Fa Miu added, "The boy has a remarkable talent for accuracy under duress, seemingly heightened when no time for thought remains."

"With the sling, the boy is matchless among the herders."

"Then you must be sure to teach him the bow."

"Yes" replied Li, "I see that now, clearly."

They finished their tea and enjoyed sweet cakes. The boy eventually joining them, obviously famished from his day of great adventure.

At one point, young Hui turned to Fa Miu and said, "Master Li told me he could get to like you if he knew you better."

The Fox nodded knowingly. The three continued in silence, light smiles evident in the glow of their faces, as they simply enjoyed their remaining time together. Enough had been said.

Fa Miu finally interjected, "It's time. The crowd has likely thinned and we should get you two on your way. The mistress brought a pouch for Master Li. She had packed the boy's mountain garb, and in the same pack made sure they both had food and sweets adequate for their journey back.

Wishing to thank the courtesy, Master Li motioned to the boy for his money purse, and the boy looked down to the floor saying nothing.

Bewildered, Li looked sternly to the boy, speechless, not wanting to question him in this memorable setting, or to embarrass him before Fa Miu.

With a gesture of his hand toward the mistress, Fa Miu made clear his intent to make her whole, she nodded understandingly and left.

The three departed, with their protectors in loose but close surround.

"One last incidental before we leave," Fa Miu said, as he guided the group back to town center, where the game makers were finalizing their accountings. Fa Miu collected handsomely on his winnings, a string of gold sovereigns which he planned to split with his two friends, but as it turned out, didn't have to.

Li Fung again held his open hand to the boy, politely signaling still again the purse be returned.

Unexpectedly, the gamesman pushed between them, calling in recognition, "Boy? Is that you? Heavens, I've been expecting you and was starting to get concerned you had disappeared. I didn't recognize you at first, where's your mountain garb? Well, never mind. First, here's your purse."

He passed Li's empty purse to Hui, who dutifully gave it over to Master Li.

"Empty?" Li said incredulously.

"And your winnings," said the gamesman, signaling his two trusties to come forward, the lead man holding a very substantial bag, struggling to manage its weight.

"Your winnings little brother. I told you I'd make a fair accounting, and here you have it."

He turned to Li Fung, "Congratulations on your noble victory, Sir. You must be very proud of the boy!"

Li had no clue what he meant, but nodded his head so as not to be disrespectful.

The child took the hide bag, and, barely able to keep his balance while managing the great weight, dropped to a squat, if only to avoid falling over. With both arms, he lifted it toward Li, "For your purse, Sir."

Even Fa Miu could not resist peering curiously over Li's shoulder as he opened the bag and stared down into five strings of gold sovereigns, coiling one around another like a den of alchemical snakes.

"You bet my life savings???!!!"

Fa Miu smiled broadly, unable to decide which impressed more, the size of the winnings, or the child's audacity. How had he managed to come into town center, find the game maker, and disappear back onto the rooftop?

Then he turned to Li, "Of course he did Master Li, who better than the boy Hui knew the likely outcome of this day's play. For him, and his innocence, a gamble anchored in complete faith."

Li looked to the boy, "We'll have to talk more of this, when there is time."

Fa Miu smiled knowingly, "Are we ready?"

Master Li and the boy nodded as one, both eager to return to their people, and their home in the near heavens.

And off they all went.

In the harsh trials which followed, few forgot how the boy's child logic had brought a small fortune to the western hills. Not enough to build a palace, or to forge an army, but just enough to carry an oppressed people through a hard year of what their oppressors planned to be an imposed starvation.

Master Li Fung, who at first had always looked upon Shi-Hui Ke as a most promising student; now viewed him as a son, so attuned in spirit had they become.

As they moved ahead through the difficult times which ensued, Li deemed it best to never again reflect sternly on the matter of his stray purse. They never discussed it further.

Book 2

The Dragon of the Midlands

Mother and Father

We search for magic, one of many compulsive yearnings in our endless race through time. Who is to say if such even exists? And if so, for what purpose? Perhaps what follows will shed a degree of light on the matter.

We look, explore, fancy and grasp. How grand if we could fly. Better yet to be invisible. How the strength of ten would quickly prove its worth, more so with the speed of the jaguar. Really now, all I ask for is enlightenment. Is that too much? Best yet if I could sniff out gold and precious gems or better still, hidden treasure. As you can see quick enough, these inclinations take on lives of their own. Our lives.

I am Shen Ling. My people have nothing but the dust beneath their worn sandals, and the promise of tomorrow's struggle when today's toils are done. Yet in that they find themselves rich in contentment, and sometimes, though absent all the wizardry and the supernatural, manage to taste joy and find completeness. But, can it be enough? Will it always satisfy? Regrettably, for many here and elsewhere, it would seem not.

My mother understood the true nature of this "magic" for which we yearn, and its tempting draw on one's imagination.

"Greed, Shen Ling. You must avoid greed."

She, above all others, knew how to cut to the marrow.

"But Ma … I was contemplating magic. Magic is wonderful, we could do the impossible, and our lives would be so enriched."

"No Shen Ling. Magic is magic. If it appears, it manifests of its own accord, but only to those who deserve to witness and to experience. What you ponder is not magic but something else which comes with hidden costs and is merely a manifestation of one's hunger for permanence and security. Careful, or no true magic will ever cross your path."

"Then you think I'm selfish?"

"No my son. Not so long as you look deeply for the fish, and don't get distracted by reflections along the water's edge. Never forget, there are many ways one can succumb to greed: the quickest lure being the quest for what removes you from your station, allowing those who should be most important to you to drift from your life and then from your thoughts. Once they're gone from your mind and heart, you'll feel only emptiness and then a gnawing hunger for something to replace what once had been yours. Hunger and greed — two most dour companions in your journey through life."

The exchange ended leaving me to ponder her words as we set about to plant rice in the rain soaked fields and to forage our evening meal; most likely frogs yet again, wild greens, bamboo, water scorpions, and if fortunate, a carp or two. Now that would be magic, short lived though it be! And of course, rice, our beautiful rice. Pure, clean, unadorned, fundamental and wholesome. A daily reminder of what made us who we are.

But it was father who truly understood greed, and could read it at a glance in the faces of others. While a child, I eavesdropped from the shadows as elders explained among themselves how he had been through, and witnessed much. For a child, it made perfect sense.

Pa never told of the imperial wars, or the subsequent rolling tides of turmoil and conflict which ebbed and flowed throughout the course of his becoming a man. His own relations struggled, and survived by treading carefully among the many competing interests, knowing there would be no future should they fail.

What competing interests? History speaks clearly to this. There may be only one Emperor, but surrounding him are those numbering beyond count who maneuver and plot to stake their own domains from whatever can be had. At first bits and pieces, then whole slabs. Worse, their imperial designs and appetites have no seeming limits, nor any concerns regarding their deleterious impact on the lives of others. Mind you, that includes the Emperor. Of course, this is nothing new. Almost to be expected, one need only study what has come before. Any period will suffice. Better yet, look with a straight eye to the present. Do that for your own good. Now! What do you see? Are the scoundrels so hard to make out? Why should anyone even bother with them? Is it any secret where it all leads? Father would caution how acknowledging them only draws you further into their game, and makes them far more important than they have any right to be. It's why empires fail, then dissipate only to be reborn from fragments and pieces to which they are again destined to return. That is our story. In due time, it will be laid bare for you.

For what it's worth, I am told by others I am the scion of warrior stock. My father's exploits were already anchored in folk tales, poems and commemoratives throughout the midlands before I ever arrived on the scene. Even in the far west, and in the remote Shu ranges, I'm told accounts linger of his past, and his heroic deeds.

I can't say whether the stories are true or not. He disdained notoriety, and never discussed the particulars of his doings. At least that's how I saw it. Others who knew more, simply acknowledged his presence and deferred to him with great reverence and respect when he entered among them.

He abhorred violence, though he was beyond question a singularly skilled martial artist. I can attest he worked the fields as well as any, understood the seasons, the cultivation and propagation of seed, planting, harvesting, caring for livestock, minding the lesser creatures, sharing with friends (human and animal), and providing for his family. He had mastered our traditions, our ways, knew how to heal, and could even cite the classics. Above all, he loved song and poetry, as did I.

He also taught us to fight. After a day fishing or working the fields we would sweat for hours beneath the still sweltering sun, working weapons, techniques, and seemingly endless forms under his probing eye. Afterward, we would soak in the pond, then sit by the evening fire singing songs of our people, sharing stories, playing our lutes, drums and whistles, or simply gazing lazily at the stars. He particularly liked my attempts at verse and I recall him smiling my way in silence whenever I recited.

Those were the best of times. Poor but fully immersed in life, embraced by community, and contented. What more could one want, or demand? Take my word on this. Those moments should be savored when you have them! Over the span of life, and history, they inevitably prove few in number, and are seldom likely to linger.

This I learned all too well; when one eventful day, he looked to the night heavens and saw how the god of war had entered into the house of domestic bliss beneath the sign of fire. He immediately consulted the Yi Ching and the concern in his eyes registered as he muttered "Po[25]," and read its promise of chaos to follow.

---

[25] Within the sacred classic, it is hexagram #23, a single solid yang line resting atop five split yin lines beneath. Referenced as splitting, imaged as destruction, or the chopping down of a tree. Thought of as disintegration from the bottom up. I like

He told us time was short. We had to push our lessons and our training to their limit. "You five children may well be our future," became his mantra.

Gregory Whincup's portrayal, "One who goes too far will be cut down. The hexagram shows someone falling from a height when his support is cut out from under him. The principal image is that of a couch collapsing when its legs are cut away." Gregory Whincup, *Rediscovering the I Ching*, (New York, St. Martin's Griffin, 1996), p.88

Disturbing Signs

My brothers Chen and Sying mastered the internal secrets of empty hand movement, along with breaking and striking. They also worked wonders with rope and cord. Nothing they tied ever came loose or undone.

My younger sisters Mayleen and An perfected the healing arts, particularly the application of herbs and remedies, and the use of needles and smoking cups to trigger energy channels and coax them to their natural flows.

Older brother Chen once told me I had been brought into the family by Pa from a distant realm in the west. Pa had been summoned there to tend to unfinished business from his past. Brother Chen recalled Ma had not been pregnant in the least, so there could be no doubt. Though himself only a child at the time, Chen remembered well my first arrival and her great surprise, might we even say, dismay? Chen said he didn't know what it all meant. Nor did I. We both swore brotherly oaths it would be our great secret, and never mentioned it again to anyone or to each other. For my siblings Sying, Mayleen and An, I had always been "gege," older brother. They had no way of knowing otherwise.

True or not, for me, Ma had been my only mother; and from the first, loved me as such; as I did her. Still, I think she would be first to say, in appearance and inclination we were different as night and day.

As to our training and our skills, all of us were well acquainted with the internal concepts, particularly the principles of non-resistance, circles, spirals, and water.

I became the master of weapons. Father said I had his gift for them.

All this to what purpose you might ask?

Pa's response to the question was always the same, "Being ready and at your best is the only life circumstance you control with certainty. Everything else falls to the whims of fate, the meddling of the immortals and the insatiable appetites of the wannabes. Of the wannabes, there are now so many in the form of warlords and renegades no one can any longer determine where legitimacy lies, or what the future holds for those like us who favor simplicity and closeness to the land."

"Pa, why tell us this. We farm, we fish, we have little. We trouble no one. Surely, this evil you see coming will pass us by and touch elsewhere. Who could possibly make anything from what little we have. Even we can't do that?"

"What I think or say means nothing. The heavens and the Oracle have spoken. Only fools would fail to take notice, and to act! In our clan, there are no fools!

"Take heed my son, this is different. Perhaps an echo, or lingering tremor from a troubled past; hopefully not a return to what we thought had been ended long ago. Regardless, they will come like a great indiscriminate plague. Even now, the scavengers lay their schemes. There (pointing to the distance as he said this) on the other side of destiny's veil. Hungry eyes already peer through. To them, we're prey, and the fodder for their ambitions. They've already made plans for us. Be still and listen carefully. One can feel it rippling in the air.

"As you say, we may have little; but signs and portents show they will be quick upon us for whatever it is they feel we are worth. We have but one choice. Today we do what must be done. Tomorrow we stand fearless, eyes open, looking straight into their faces as they come upon us. They won't have seen that before. I will prepare you and ensure you are capable and ready, just as did my grandfather and my many mentors for me. Those who come will never anticipate peasants like us joining the dance of chaos as welcoming participants. We'll render full account for who we are and where we stand relative to their sinister aims."

His words proved achingly true. Before season's end, our livestock and stores were ravaged by the passing armies and their minions. And it went deeper down from there. Daughters, sisters, wives and mothers were violated, beaten, shamed and abused. Young males were pulled into service, children programed to spy or worse, and young ladies of promise ill served. Families flew to the four directions like dust lifted by a ghastly wind. Our once village remained only as a shell emptied of its former self, devoid of life, but for stragglers, beggars, the elderly and the infirm.

Ma disappeared one day. She had gone discreetly about to forage some greens. She went alone so as not to draw undue attention. To no avail, father had warned her never to do so. We were told a band of soldiers took her off to be a camp slave. I can't say more of it, or what it means. Even now the words choke in my throat. We scoured and searched for the turn of two moons but, likely fearing for their own safety, no one would tell us anything more. Simply gone. We never saw her again, though her compassionate and kind spirit remained ever alive within our memories. Among ourselves, we held a funeral. We knew she would not allow herself to be abused or shamed.

Mounting numbers of bodies were reposited to rot in fields to the south. There, night winds blew away from the village, now occupied by the intruders; but the stench filled the countryside. We searched constantly, as much as we could bear, too often finding friends and relations cut from existence then discarded. Did we complain? Did we protest? Of course. "Coincidental losses of war" we were told by the bastards in charge. "Unavoidable" tragedies. Or, when the bolder among us demanded accountability or explanation, "This is what happens to fools who lack the simple sense to stay the hell out of the way."

Those who complained to the lords in hopes of finding some degree of understanding and compassion typically received three coppers in consolation. A token, which though not expected, beat nothing at all; seeming to some degree a measure of acknowledgment for their concern, or perhaps a polite gesture of empathy. Only to themselves disappear after having been marked by their supposed benefactors as "More problems to be reconciled. You'll know them by the coppers in their purse."

Father dispatched the five of us into the surrounding hills, ordering we must survive for the future, and for hope's sake. He assured we had learned all we needed to know, gave us his love, then turned about, walking alone and straight for where they were, assuring as he walked away he would buy ample time for our escape.

He faded from our view then blended into their midst, wreaking terrible havoc on the contemptuous interlopers.

It's not easy for anyone to break ties to family, home and past; even if it means survival. That's how it was for me. On occasion, I would steal back and venture near our once homestead to see if I could find Pa, or even glimpse the ghost of my mother. Selfishly, I thought to find him there lingering among the shadows, hopefully tempted to emerge joyfully on realizing my approach.

There would be nothing, only encroaching outsiders squatting over what had been ours, having their own way with what remained from our lives. Even the simple village, once center of our youthful joy, had begun to stink like rotting manure.

However, my spirits lifted on learning from the whispering few who remained that when darkness fell, mysterious events unfolded. There would be screams of agony and horrible death yells throughout the night, conflagrations would erupt spontaneously, cavalry horses would run in terror from the village to the surrounding hills as soldiers searched frantically but pointlessly for the cause. In the morning one could see carts full of soldiers' lifeless corpses being wheeled toward the south where now only the death pit seemed capable of producing any substantive harvest.

I knew then Pa lived still. The many stories and accounts I once heard from the village elders echoed on the troubled countenances of the occupying officers.

Soon enough, the surrounding hill folk began singing new songs of honor and recognition to the reincarnated "Dragon of the Midlands" who once again reconciled the peasants' ledger, demanding full recompense against the account of all uninvited intruders. In the countryside, spirits lifted, and I then came to understand father's directive that we were the best prospect for hope and a future. The peasants recalled how once in the distant past, the enormous yoke of oppression had been lifted. They sensed a new promise it would be lifted again. Some even took up arms.

All because of Bao Ling. My Pa!

I might have lingered forever, or until I somehow came upon him. I well would have, but for an unmistakable sign he left for my sole benefit.

Closing out yet another futile search, I awoke as morning sun peeked hesitatingly over evening's darkened cover to find what looked to be my father's bow lying by my side, along with a generous number of his carefully crafted arrows. I knew from what others passed in their accounts that once a great master had gifted a divine bow to the noble Dragon of the Midlands. To my father! For most, it was just another story, an embellishment, but this story had meat on its bone.

I had seen it!

In its magnificence, the bow stood as the embodiment of perfection.

He rarely showed it, and few believed it existed. That was all the better for Pa. Why tempt the unworthy or the carelessly curious? Worse yet, should it ever fall into the wrong hands!

As I grew from youth, Pa took great care to teach me the bow maker's craft. On rare occasions, he would lay this particular specimen before me; explaining it to be singular; adding few had ever set eyes upon such a masterpiece of art, form and function.

For most, at distance, it looked to be an ordinary bow, though possessing elements of subtlety and craft which compelled one to study it closely. Only when holding it in one's hands and examining with bow fitter's eyes could the fine intricacies be appreciated.

Father believed a craftsman could never replicate something he had not seen, or even knew was possible to exist. It was for that reason he afforded me the opportunity to hold it and learn its subtleties for myself. I remember how it surprised father that I could lift it. He said many could not, "If the Dragon didn't find you worthy, it would resist your even holding it." Might that have been the "magic" mother alluded to?

The aspiring craftsman had only his "best" in any given moment, which was fine if your intent was to shoot birds flocking in fields; quite a difference from holding back the tide when chaos threatened. With a bit of luck and diligent effort, a self-evolved craftsman could fabricate enough bows over the course of a lifetime that trial after error would eventually start guiding his hand to evolve his craft, so long as he had an impeccable attitude. Impeccable attitude; Pa's mantra. We can never be perfect, but with an "impeccable attitude" we would always be stepping in the right direction, and were assured through that commitment to find our very best in each moment. "Someday son, I will uncover the secrets within this bow. When I do, perhaps I'll fashion another." I remember him looking my way as he said it, but knew not to let my hopes run away with my imagination.

From this clear message delivered to my hands, I never expected to see him again. When they saw it for themselves, my siblings somberly agreed. We had only his words and his lessons to cling to, along with what he expected of us.

And now, in my hands, his painstaking replication of the Dragon Bow …

His wishes were clear.

A Father's Gift

Bow making is an exacting art, and a bow like this, properly conceived and constructed, can perform extraordinary feats. Its fabrication combined antelope horn, mulberry wood, wild deer sinew and spruce. The materials were carefully trimmed, glued and laminated to create a miracle of efficiency. The belly, facing the archer, was horn, behind a wooden core, with sinew stretched along the outside. The ends curved back in stylized elegance, not so discretely masking the power, insertions of bone and antler reinforced the tips. The hide glue appeared to come from the usual sources, though I suspect Pa would have preferred the bladders of large fish for this particular effort. He always felt there was "magic in the construct." If done properly, a mutualism might be found which resonated with the spirit of the archer. In bows we fashioned together, finding the materials sometimes took months. Constructing, gluing, laminating, and finishing took even longer. This one, judging it against the master, likely took a lifetime.

The original Dragon Bow is a composite bow, exquisite in its construction. Mine too was a masterpiece, and but for the one it emulated without peer. From a step or two away, it looked to be quite ordinary, I'm sure father intended it that way. It wasn't until you held it in your hands and sensed its spirit when its uniqueness could be appreciated. Only then might you trace your fingers over its length and width taking in the extraordinary complexity of its fabrication, marveling at the seemingly disparate elements somehow integrating perfectly into a miracle of craft.

On our referring to the original, he stressed, "Son, study it closely. Only hands which have passed through many lifetimes can combine so many materials in such a way that each acts to push the other beyond its natural limitations, in effect yielding a device which challenges all preconceived notions and expectations."

In size, it was not large, not quite 5 chi[26]. I am somewhat tall. From tip to tip, when strung, it would scarcely reach my chest. It could comfortably be carried slung diagonally over the body, and facilitated riding on horseback, traversing difficult terrain, or even climbing trees. On horseback, one could take the bow, and easily turn completely to the rear to fire with crippling force at an armored attacker. With enemies to the front, it fared even better.

----

[26] A unit of measurement referred to as the "Chinese foot." The precise length can vary depending on both locale and historical time period. Currently it is generally accepted to be 1/3 of a meter. During the period of the story, it would have measured approximately 9.5 inches.

The obvious intent of the design, and the materials chosen was to create great power in a transportable parcel of moderate size. While the front flexed and stretched, the rear compressed and stored the energy until released.

We frequently made wood bows for our casual use, usually of yew, maple or even bamboo. They were fine bows, but their arrows would never pierce armor. I had witnessed father shooting. For his bow, no problem. I'll soon tell you more of that.

I named my new bow "Sleeping Dragon," recalling the spirit of its inspiration, and because its peerless nature evoked for me the image of the fabled Chancellor Zhuge Liang, and bespoke its potential. And also because no one knew of its existence, or its potency. At least not while it slept in readiness.

Beneath the beauty and character of my Sleeping Dragon, secrets whispered from the dawn of warfare.

The Straw Man

Father's Dragon Bow. How can one even speak of it in a meaningful sense? Words fail to convey its essence or its nobility.

Doubtless, its pedigree would place it among the greatest in the land. I for one have seen no equal, nor have I ever heard of one.

You might think one great bow much the same as any other. Perhaps, but one single characteristic sets this specimen far apart from its peers. In the hands of the right person, it can reach the unreachable.

When we trained together, Pa referred to it as "One-Li[27]" as least as often as he called it the Dragon Bow. It seemed

---

[27] Li is commonly thought of as the "Chinese mile." Today, in the People's Republic, it represents 500 meters. Historically, the length varied. During the period of our story, it would have been approximately 400 meters, sometimes more, sometimes less.

the Bow had a proper name, and a casual name, One-Li being the informal, and spoken as if of a friend. Puzzled, I would ask, "Why One-Li father? Why two names?"

Father answered, "Dragon is for the ears of others, so they know of its authority and are cautioned of the consequences for crossing purposes with it. One-Li is for the soul of its partner and master. Only a select few can waken the Dragon within, and ride the potential to its celestial peak. Don't you think they've earned the privilege of familiarity?"

He had me there. For the longest time, he would say nothing further. I remained stuck on that thought for years, puzzling over the depth of its true meaning.

As he aged, and the storm clouds began to clot the flow of our destinies, he determined the moment had come to reveal for me the Bow's greatest secret, and why he referred to it as One-Li.

From the outset, it was not to be our typical evening of practice. Already, probes and vanguards hinting at legions in waiting came to spy on our humble surrounds. Villagers reported seeing them everywhere, meticulously mapping and surveying resources. How carefully they noted the availability of able bodies, hatching plans for new brigades of coerced labor along with anything else of strategic worth. Those fellows could see nothing, but how and what to exploit. At first, they came in modest clusters, pretending to be wanderers or peasants. To us, they stood out like wolves in a barn. Definitely not natural or common to the surround. Certainly, not wanted or welcomed.

Notable for their constant questions, their hungry eyes roved eager to take measure of all, particularly when their volatile senses read what might be discerned as threats. For that reason, to ensure safety our practice sessions drifted further and further from the village, avoiding their relentless scrutiny. Often as not this mandated we return late in the evening stumbling along through darkness, or sometimes in the early morning, all the more worn and weary. This truly tasked our stamina, capping off an already full day working the fields, gathering food and tending livestock. Even then, though early in the occupation, we were deemed suspects. The "fire star"[28] inclined toward chaos, and suspicion remained its close ally. Besides, there was Pa's reputation, which in spite of neighbors' efforts at discretion and secrecy, still drew unwanted attention our way, if only because no one would speak directly about him or his past, except to say he came from a line of peasant farmers and kept to himself and his own. What else could they say, or do? They preferred to guard their tongues. Times being what they were, the spies only became more suspicious from this, and hovered about our surrounds all the more obvious for their laughable efforts to avoid detection. They marked, studied and reported our every move. It might have struck absurdly funny had it not been so deadly serious.

Still, it was our domain, and we determined when we were seen, and when we were not. On this particular occasion, we ventured far into the hills, ensuring isolation

---

[28] The planet Mars. It's ominous influence doubtless part of what Bao Ling considered in declaring "The heavens and the Oracle have spoken."

from busy eyes. There we rested and nourished ourselves in the welcoming quiet and emptiness. Father searched for a spot where we could work discretely. He carefully surveyed the locale, noting the positions of trees, rises, streams and trails intent on ruling out the possibility of eavesdroppers.

He then fabricated a target, a straw man, which he positioned upright, hidden deep within a grove of cypress trees. Concerned, I asked, "Pa do we want the target here, in the middle of these ancient trees?" Frankly, we felt a spiritual connection to the cypress. They populated our swamps and stood vigilant like wizened beings guarding our wetlands. They had been there as long as anyone knew. The presence of their spirits could be sensed as we moved about. Timeless beings, aware of everything. It may seem silly, but for us, no less than extended family.

"They're not at risk son. We'll be careful for them. No one would expect our target to be placed here, and it will be safe from prying eyes."

Once the target was set, father attached an armored plate, metal nearly thick as my thumb over what would have been its chest. Then with his hand blade, he scribed a small circle marking where would have been the straw heart behind it. Next, he shaped a crude head, mounting it above the plate, and cut within what seemed a hesitant grin. He capped it with moss for good measure. Its smile seemed forced and doubly artificial.

Laughing at his efforts, I said, "Father, even with the grin, I would say this was not a happy man, or even one to be trusted."

He turned to me, "Yes, perhaps like us, he senses what lies in store. He tells us it's now every dummy for himself. In that regard, an honest dummy; a skeptic. Let's go!"

"Where to?"

"To find our shooting position."

We trekked for some time, cutting through the bush and wetland, then around some rocky fingers, and finally over a small but robust stream where we took great care not to lose footing against the capricious current. All the while Dragon rested, already strung and slung cross-body over his shoulder, accompanied by father's tightly packed quiver of arrows. Constantly looking back to check, I knew we had already drifted far out of range. I didn't see any purpose to continuing our efforts, especially considering the risks.

After going some additional distance, we stopped to rest. It grew late. I looked to father, my countenance questioning his intent. He turned, "Are you ready?"

"What am I to be ready for?" Before I finished, he was already standing, arrow mounted, bow in hand. The quickness surprised me. I wouldn't say he moved fast, so much as smoothly. Deliberate, measured, and sure footed. It seemed more as though his quickness came unexpectedly, always evoking surprise, even though I had witnessed it many times. When he moved, nothing lay wasted, and all effort served his singular purpose. I know it now to be an art perfected through endless challenges survived over a lifetime. No resistance impeded his flow. Simply clean movement, so simple in fact, it could not be replicated or matched by the countless others who had so often tried yet failed.

Then he froze motionless. I knew his intent, and told him he'd be wasting a good arrow, then just as quickly questioned why? I saw no purpose to it. He proceeded to quiet his spirit, smelling, and listening, noting the movement of birds in flight, the bouncing of insects, ripples on the creek, and the quiet but ever present breath of conscious reality, sitting just beneath our mundane images of perception. The wind crawled about like a serpent in its native element, always winding its dance, just beyond the limits of familiar awareness. Not so for Pa. He was mimicking the cobra, purging distraction, relaxing into the surround. That very stillness rippled outward from his center in an ever expanding arc of purpose toward our front.

I saw nothing; no target. Doubtless we had ventured too far from the straw man. I could not see, nor say what he took aim upon. Somewhere in the far distance, the straw man stood safely concealed and protected within the grove of cypress. Fact is, I couldn't even remember the direction, still disoriented from our haphazard cross country jaunt. Had that been his plan?

From within father's stillness, his exhalation through the bow rocketed the arrow forward heading to points uncertain. Something new, I completely lost sight of it on release! A most mighty shot indeed!

I looked questioningly at him. He smiled my way, effortlessly stringing a second shaft. This he let loose in an instant. If I had blinked, I would have missed the interval between the two releases.

Thinking it wasteful, I couldn't resist pointing out, "Seems to me if a person spent a good part of an evening crafting and balancing arrows to impeccable precision, he'd be a lot more careful about dim lighting and losing them in the brush."

"There. Now, you'll see the first shot wasn't simply luck."

"And what is it we're talking about? You lost me back at the straw man. The sun's already down, evening star coming into view, I'm chilled, and we'll never find our way out tonight. It's too dark even to practice. But for our pleasant walk, a wasted day."

"No matter, we'll set a warm but careful fire and ponder the stars and destiny. The straw man can bide time till morning."

We were up at first light, rekindled the fire, and ate as we warmed. I wouldn't have found my way back to the cypress grove without father's careful prompting in reading signs left by our prior day's movements. I had my own skills in tracking. For him it was second nature. In fact, we often joked he could read signs of movement better than he could make sense of written characters. A bent leaf, an incorrect shadow, ripples in a muddy swirl, the track of an animal suddenly shifting weight or changing directions, debris, human soil, all told their bits of tale, which, when threaded together in the mind of an artist, spoke of directions, armament, numbers, animals, and sometimes hinted at ultimate intent.

It seemed to take even longer getting back to the straw man; I didn't realize just how many turns our original trek had taken. By midmorning, the cypress grove reemerged into our view, and I could finally see the straw man patiently lingering in the distance, still tempting our attack. Not waiting for father's order, I stopped, readied my bow, set a shaft, then stalked through the surrounding brush.

Father laughed, "No need for that. This straw man has already served his purpose."

I returned to his full view, puzzled. He signaled for me to move forward, and I followed his lead. As we neared the straw man, I saw father's first arrow sticking from the circle etched in its armored breast plate.

The second was centered in its smile, originally circumspect and almost a sneer, now more a grimace as ends of straw displaced and drooped from its sides.

Staring in disbelief, I murmured, "How is this possible?" I moved even closer to convince myself the wizardry was not some artful trick or stunt. Indeed, defying all expectations, the metal plate had been punctured.

But no dissemblance proved evident. I scoured the surrounds for any sign of others who might have helped Pa set up the deception on me. The area proved clean, nothing, but for our own signs of activity barely visible from the previous day.

Then he spoke, "Shen Ling, among the bows of the world, Dragon is supreme. She was gifted to me by the great master Sying Hao in friendship and in recognition of my archery and my nurturing under his tutelage. Until I met Master Hao, I had used only bows I could fabricate from the local woods. They were generally simple bows, but effective; mostly because I had from necessity elevated my craft to where it became an art. Master Hao first found me one morning as I stood alone taking aim with one of my creations, testing the glide of differing lengths of bamboo shafts, and the effect of differing vanes on their spin.

"Early on I had found ways to challenge my skills which went far beyond typical archer's practice. At some point, I steered away from stationary targets, and static positions. When possible, always careful not to draw unwanted attention, I would ride mounted, or standing in the back of a cart, often piloted by my friend Old Jou who would zig and zag, race and slow through the back roads. In time, even that became predictable, and less of a challenge. Then one spring the locusts came, following upon the rains. It proved to be an opportunity. As you know, locusts plague our existence. One never knows what will follow when they first appear. You need only experience one scourge to appreciate their immense and unforgiving hunger. You've seen yourself, they are wary creatures, and can sense your intent on approach. It's no wonder they survive efforts to destroy them. Reach down to cup one in your hands. As you close on your target he will suddenly spring and break angle, usually off to your side or over one of your shoulders and to your rear. This is of course a great skill, programmed by thousands of generations having to survive in hostile environments. For me, it was their small size, their quickness and their unpredictability which made them attractive as targets in advancing my efforts. Though I try to avoid wanton destruction of life, locusts for one fell outside my compassion. I knew their potential for destruction from hard experience, and felt I was doing our crops and people a service by lessening their numbers. Besides, the game was fair.

"At first I tried shooting them from a few feet away. Before long, I realized my arrow's shaved stone tip was working against my intent, actually pushing them aside as the shaft passed. I devised special blunt tips to better suit my purpose. It took a considerable long time, but as I remember, by midsummer I had hit my first. Intentionally, that is. By that I mean there was one with distinctive yellow eyes, set well off from the red and green of his companions. Those eyes drew my aim to him, and from a distance of 15 chi[29], I knocked him from the air. No exaggeration, I had probably taken over ten thousand shots those several months, and smashed countless arrows. There are no words adequate to express my mounting frustration or my release from its grip once I tasted first success. Certainly, before that, there were the occasional lucky hits, but they meant nothing. I couldn't bank luck among the assets in my arsenal. Be grateful for luck when you have it Shen Ling, but never count on it. I required conscious certainty. Already, storm clouds were brewing to the east, and there were whispers and expectations of turmoil to come. I planned to be ready.

---

[29] About 5 big steps.

"It was a great relief to choose one, and to hit the one I chose. Not surprisingly, I could not repeat the feat that day, or the next, or the next. But, one week later, a red eyed demon alighted from some sorghum and as he ascended, I drew my shaft and fired without even a thought. He dropped instantly to the ground.

"In the months which followed, the hits became more frequent and certain. In a year's time, while standing, I could select and hit a locust anywhere within 30 paces. Eventually it was 50 paces, beyond that, I could no longer see them individually. Still, the improvement in my skill was evident, and I, for one, grew satisfied the long effort had proven worth the while. Certainly, no others I knew or heard of could better it. Yet even with that, contentment eluded me. The thought nagged. I wondered if I might yet push it even further.

"At that stage, I enlisted Old Jou back into the game. Again, I tried shooting from his moving cart as he coursed through the fields. But now, locusts were the targets. Believe me, hitting a locust from a moving cart is no easy undertaking. Worse still, complications double should the creature go airborne. Quickly humbled, I returned to square one. Only this time, the trajectory to achievement followed more quickly than before. Trust me on this, success breeds success. You can build on your accomplishments, they will prove sturdy as a vessel, like a deck beneath your feet no matter what challenges lie before you. For that reason above all others, strive for perfection in all you do. And that's what I did. Hoping to polish the evolving skill to still higher sheen, I commandeered Jou's horse. I again re-visited the exercise one final time, only now executing while mounted.

"By then, I was three years down the path. Hell had begun to unleash its furies, and vandals came upon us from all four directions. Nothing seemed to make sense. Unlike locusts, these hosts, because of their blatant arrogance and disregard, were much easier to see and bring down. And I did. Best of all, I didn't have to seek them out. They found me.

"It's like that you know, the more you try to get out of their way, the stronger your scent settles into their nostrils. I tried to escape their attention first as a common hunter, then as woodsman, and failed. As with the locusts, I saw them for the plague they were, and performed my tasks with clear determination I would survive, our people would survive. At their expense if such proved necessary, particularly if they didn't have the courtesy and good sense to simply let things be."

"Strive for perfection
in all you do."

Meeting Sying Hao

I listened to him intently, thinking only one thing. He had never mentioned "Sying Hao" to any of us before that day.

I remember how he said the name. Almost like a mantra, or a whispered prayer, perhaps a call of hope for an old friend who might respond from nothingness and yet again appear. My interest piqued, I begged father tell me of this master who thought well enough of him to bestow such a precious gift.

It turned out they shared much more than the Dragon Bow. Sying Hao had been teacher and older brother to my father at a time when, as now, the world began to inexplicably turn upon itself. His masterly hand on everything which followed their first encounter had been profound (you'll learn more of that at another time). As to why father never mentioned him? Perhaps the memory weighed too heavily, and could not be lightly spoken.

I suspect for that reason, he at first resisted, reluctant to humor my curiosity. Then with time and due reflection, stirred no doubt by my persistence, he eventually succumbed. Smiling politely, his face assuming an air of resignation, he recalled how, "Sying Hao came upon me for the first time while I tested new shafts on some locusts. By then, I had already skirmished with the war lords. Understand, they came and went at will with their toadies, respecting no bounds of propriety. Don't get me wrong. I didn't stalk them. As a rule I don't seek out victims, or kill the unwary. Most were once people just like us; regrettably turned about and now facing away. We mustn't forget that! They came to serve war lords because they had no options or alternatives, apart from feeling useless, hopeless, afraid and deprived. It's not so illogical to accept the accommodation of dealing it to others as a better place to be than having it dealt to you. So much of life is like that. Mere practicality. Accommodation keeps you and those important to you away from unwanted trouble, but it lasts for only a fleeting moment. Never forget that. It's a fool's bargain.

"I had also been approached by them, even had opportunity to meet their chieftains. Those guys weren't ignorant. If anything, their intelligence impressed me as being far more sophisticated than my own. Perhaps I should say complicated, or more precisely, devious. Within them a frightening philosophy of life and existence somehow took strong root, and ran their thoughts counter to all I deemed real, true, and sacred. In trying to enlist me, they would brazenly proclaim for my edification how the world was in fact already 'hell' and I owed it to myself, my family and loved ones to recognize this single essential reality. Once I did that, everything else would become crystal clear! 'Learn to manipulate it to full advantage Bao Ling, there's no telling how fast you can rise, or how high. You have real potential young man! Join us, that's where your future lies. What better alternatives do you see out there?'

"I refused to play their game. With what politeness I could muster, I told them the world wasn't 'hell' and despite their best efforts to make it so, the Tao and Dharma would in the end hold all twisted courses to true account, as had been the case so often in the past. They laughed at what they called my superstitious nature, challenging me to show them the Tao and Dharma of which I spoke. They reminded how everything they had was real, and acquired through discipline, hard work, and courage pitted against considerable odds. How could I, an untested person with nothing, argue with that.

"Clearly, what I did possess and value they could no longer see. Nor could they receive it, even if I gave it freely to them. I'm embarrassed to say, hearing them, and seeing their conviction, I even began to doubt myself.

"Of course, what I did say signaled to them I needed a touch of their special persuasion. If not with them in spirit, by default I had become a threat. They set a price on my capture. Then, when they couldn't capture me, an even higher price on my head. Rightfully figuring I couldn't be turned, they wanted me gone from the board. In their own words; 'Resistance is pointless! You'll be our proof by example!' When first they said that to me, I laughed and replied, 'Exactly. Once you come to grips with that, you'll understand your way of hell can only fail. Why, it's nothing but resistance, a speck pushing against life's eternal flow.

Why don't we all agree to disagree and spare those around us the games and suffering during the interim?'

"They didn't like that either. As for those they sent to learn me, I honestly tell you, we were sure to soon meet. For I wasn't going anywhere. I would exist right here, atop the hallowed ground where lay our ancestors.

"But I had to be cautious, alert and smart. I took to the wilderness and assumed the ways of the wild. In not too long a time, my natural survival skills emerged heightening my already keen senses, particularly my instincts regarding threat and danger. In many ways, I became like any other wild creature, skills sharpened to where I invariably could hear, even smell when others approached. All long before they knew I was in the neighborhood.

"But Sying Hao, his instincts? What can I say? He was already upon me before even my shocked surprise.

"I turned quickly toward him, bow drawn, arrow in the ready, tip waiting to lift his way, 'Friend or enemy?' "

I Never Joke About My Art

"He responded, 'A great archer would be able to nail them at 100 paces, a singular archer, at 200 paces, and an archer for the ages, at 300.' He was referring to the locusts of course. He came upon me in the midst of my practicing.

" 'I can do 50 paces most times, not always. No further, and I know of no one better. As to 300 paces, we both know an arrow will sail true only so far.'

" 'May I?' he asked, extending his hand to inspect my bow.

"I hesitated for a moment, wary, then supposed had he been an enemy he would have finished me off long before I ever saw him. I passed the bow and shaft, which he took and studied carefully.

" 'You made these?'

" 'Yes.'

" 'You have come a long way in your craft. Who taught you?'

" 'My grandfather guided my early efforts. Then with him gone, time, frustration, mistakes, blunders, corrections, failures, successes. All became my teachers.'

" 'And so they are ultimately for all of us. Still, one can skirt failure and needless frustration with proper guidance. Clearly you have benefited from some kindly influences.'

"I nodded in agreement, warm remembrances of grandfather, his fellows, and times past.

" 'May I try it?'

" 'I'd consider it a privilege to hear your thoughts on it, sir.' I passed him my quiver.

"With expert hand he checked the tension on the bow, then set an arrow to ready as we stepped off what he reckoned to be a hundred paces. He turned, and asked, 'Which would you like me to hit?'

"I begged off, 'No jokes good sir, we are too far off to pick one, let alone see one in the brush. Go ahead and take a different target.'

" 'Then I will select the red eyed one, there, in the distance, measuring the length of my thumb.'

"He turned from me, then quickly flew his shot. I could tell nothing with certainty, except that the shaft struck a protruding boulder, then shattered. I'm sure I winced at the loss of yet another arrow.

"He noticed of course, 'My apologies, I'll fashion a replacement for you before we part.'

" 'No need sir, I would not wish to impose on your good will.'

" 'At the least, would you be so kind as to test my result?'

" 'Indeed, my very thought.'

"Together, we went to the boulder. On approach, I saw he had in fact struck a locust, driving it's body hard into the stone. The creature, thorax crushed, lay at the base, I reached down and saw its dead red eyes, lifted it, then held it against the archer's thumb. It was as he said."

" 'You think I was lucky, perhaps?'

" 'I think nothing sir, except I could not have done your shot without the benefit of luck.'

" 'What would settle the issue?'

" 'For me, it needn't be settled. You did what you said to do, I already suspect you are a better archer than I.'

" 'Perhaps if I can repeat it at 200 paces, you will be so generous as to share a meal with this famished intruder?'

" 'Well spoken friend. A meal would be well deserved, if offered in payment for such a miracle. May I be so bold as to choose. There, on that stalk, midway, one rests apart from the others, its eyes like rainbows.'

"He took careful note, pointed 'that one,' then looked to me for affirmation. The bargain was set. As we walked away, he joked over whether the creature would be so patient as to hold steady for the convenience of his shot.

"I responded, 'Sometimes they do, sometimes they don't. Does it matter? I doubt we'll know either way. At 200 paces he'll be invisible to us.'

" 'It depends on how you see my friend, and on how you understand what you look at.'

"After stepping the 200 paces, he turned, took measure, and shot. The arrow veered high and to the left, what I considered to be an errant attempt. I gave him my raised 'told you so' flash of eyebrow accented with a tilt of my head, and we quietly started back. I reckoned no shot taken so casually could ever hit a target at that distance.

"As we neared, he turned to me and said, 'So there's no error in your final assessment, he left the stalk just as I let the arrow fly, only to meet his doom attempting to catch the breeze.'

" 'Seriously?'

" 'Seriously. I never joke about my art.'

" 'Then show me your dead locust with rainbow eyes.'

"He walked to a spot 4 paces left, and 5 steps back from the stalk, then squatted to the ground and pointed. 'Here! Your locust wishes to greet you.'

"And in fact, there it lay, the arrow was well beyond, having continued its trajectory.

"I looked to him, 'Part of me calls it luck, part of me stands in awe and amazement. All of me struggles with how?'

" 'Shall I try at 300 paces?'

" 'No, I've seen enough. Besides, you are already at the weapon's limit. Your account with me is settled. Let's share the meal you've justly earned. I am Bao Ling of the Ling village, a humble nobody, except that I work very hard at it. And you honorable sir, what is your distinguished name?' "

And Who Do You Serve?

" 'Ah *Bao Ling*. I've heard your name on the lips of soldiers. Seems you've earned a reputation for interfering with their plans and for raiding their stores. From testaments along the trail, it's clear they fear you, and wish you soon gone.'

" 'I want no bad blood or dishonor between us big brother, or lies. I do what I do, and usually for good reason. What I take is returned in one form or another to the poor, from whom it was stolen. As you can see, I am not a wealthy man, nor do I crave undeserved influence or power. Others sport their accoutrements, not I. I pray I am not perhaps another locust about to enter your sights.'

"Long silence, 'No, I am of myself, and not for anyone's hire. I am Sying Hao of the Southern Mountain. I live a quiet life, pretty much alone. By choice ... surrounded by the things which interest me. Once, I was young like you, saw and did much, but now am getting older, and have long since grown beyond the nonsense which drives men to foolishness. I don't include you in that assessment little brother. I can see already, we are cut from common fabric. As to how I come to be here? Curiosity perhaps. I thought to take a walk. Travel the great land. Peek yet again into the affairs of humankind. I hoped to see if things had changed, perhaps improved, since I first began my retreat.'

"Southern Mountain! Can you imagine that? How far had he wandered? What had he learned?

" 'Have they?'

"He looked to the ground and spit, 'Of course not! What was I thinking? Ambition, selfishness, greed; emptied of compassion and restraint. Change? Not! Great demons seem ever to roam this land, dispossessing the spirits of whomsoever they will, whenever they will. They follow their own seasons, not unlike the locusts. Reaching far outward in their spring; harvesting in their autumn; then consolidating their bounty for the winter's lull, where they scheme endless plots to follow.'

"We smiled wryly toward one another. It's rare to have someone in front of you who fully understood. I sensed then, we could become fast friends.

"In a few moments, we cleared a space, made our fire, then dined to humble contentment in silence. Afterwards, unable to resist, even to the point of risking impoliteness, I questioned him regarding his shots. I had assumed at 100 paces, he was still able to somehow see what I could not. But I wasn't sure. Only one way to find out. There exist quirks of nature and oddities among individuals. Some have eyes like eagles, I count myself among them; others like bats. Even for eyes of an eagle, the shot at 200 paces was miraculous. By my reckoning, Sying Hao proved to be possessed of supreme skill. Any insights he deemed fit to share would be beyond my lowly deserving. So, politeness aside, deserving or not, I pushed selfishly forward.

" 'If your question is whether I saw the first with my eyes, as you normally do, I can say no. I did however know he was there long before we walked away, just as I knew of the others you might have chosen. I've learned to leave nothing to chance. When I readied to shoot, all I saw was a field of red, pulsating in the distance. When we agreed on the red-eyed one for the test, I tied a thought to his thorax, and I fashioned that thought with the color of his eyes. No reason for this, it's just how I do it, and experience has shown it to work. When I turned and sighted the field of red, I could see it remained stationary, and that it felt no inclination to move. I had time to measure the shot, the distance, and the effects of the environment. With your own considerable skill, you know even the wisp of air from the wings of a butterfly can trick an arrow from its course. Incomprehensible though it may seem, but true nonetheless, everything is interconnected. The rustling fur on a coyote is somehow tied to the flip of an eagle's wing, and anchored within the subtle wriggle of an earth worm making its way delicately below. Some of this you already know from your history of practice and the lessons gleaned. Have you never felt to be on the very edge of time and perception, just as you were about to release your arrow to some impossible target in the distance? How did you manage to tighten that line, to find what lay within the arrow's potential?'

" 'Big brother, I am a simple and some would say a poorly informed man. I know the ways of the land and of my people, and I am blessed with our traditions, our stories, and our shared hopes. But the unknown, such as the things beyond time and perception of which you speak would be lost on a simpleton like me. I wouldn't have a clue if I were seeing it when I saw it.'

" 'You take yourself too lightly my friend, even while you carry the weight of battle for the midlanders. I've been mindful of what you are doing, your growing reputation already casts a long shadow. It's a hard lonely road full of sacrifice, uncertainty, and scarcity. Have you never considered attaching to one of the warlords? Who knows, you might even change them? Most certainly, they'd reward your skills handsomely.'

"Laughing, I looked at him incredulously, 'No, their largesse would be wasted on this peasant. Besides, it just wouldn't sit well with me; my stomach turns even at the thought. Not now, not in a thousand lifetimes. Cater to their quenchless desires, or plow misery through the world to justify self serving ends? I say again. No! My going with them would only further embolden their ways and draw others like me into their fold. I am a tree which likes its own roots, and craves no others. Content where I stand. That's me. Better I wasn't born than to become like them. I may be simple, but this I believe. What little I comprehend will only push to the proper mark through my direct actions, and my efforts to manifest compassion. I am the alternate to them, the counter thrust in waiting. Nature dictates I, and others like me, exist, and I accept that, though it comes with many tests. No matter of choice, I can see no other way. Yin's dot

in their field of Yang. That leaves little room for unbridled
desire.'

"Nodding, Sying Hao affirmed he understood, then
carefully added, 'Last week, I came across the bodies of three
soldiers, with arrows of your fashion protruding from their
necks. Was that your compassion?'

" 'Perhaps in the quickness of execution. Perhaps in the
fact had they not first drawn on me, I would have passed
them uneventfully. Is it wrong to cut the head off a
poisonous snake when it strikes first at you? Look at them
and who they were. I won't deny, they deserved pity.
Provide a weapon or a uniform and paint some baubles on a
starving and otherwise hapless fellow, and you have already
stirred the whims of oppression and domination into his
nature. Who would dare chance where that leads, and in the
end feel right about it? No less than being possessed by a
demon. Nudge him a bit further and you'll have a heartless
killer waiting only for your bidding. Why, even those who
make them, begin to fear them.'

" 'Warlords, generals, even kings and emperors do what
they do. Just like me. We all have our beliefs, our
principles. Then they brazenly create their own histories
and ethics, hoping to prove conclusively their renderings
were in fact driven, guided, or motivated by the righteous
will of heaven. Meanwhile, those like me, maybe you too,
become their villains. What you and I know to have been
evil, is somehow spun into golden good when their stories
are finally scrolled, and the next generation is once again
blinded to the reality, sadly setting the stage for all to repeat
once more. That's why I love the folk songs and tales of my

people. No falsehood there! As to my own dilemma? There is no easy release, I roam this wilderness by choice. I cannot be of their world, and they allow me no other! Would-be emperors fighting like mad dogs for pieces of crumbling dynasties. Warlords sectioning slabs from rotting carcasses, and we, always victims, forever exploited. Our children and kin indentured to serve, or facilitate, or worse yet, anchor the battle fronts of their audacity. I truly don't understand it. I can't harbor those inclinations within myself so I look with astonishment, confusion, and sorrow at what I see. Change them by joining? Never! At best, I would be an impediment if ever allied to a warlord or some aspiring king or emperor. A stick always in their throat. A painful tooth bellowing in the face of their yearnings.'

" 'So, here I am for the fleeting moment, a distraction indeed, but a free man.'

"Sying Hao laughed, 'To the contrary, my friend. You would be their esteemed jewel. Why, if they could convert you, they could win anyone over!'

" 'Fortunately, we are all safe from that. And you, Sying Hao, who do you serve?'

" 'Serve little brother? I've already said I'm too old for games and nonsense. I've long known warlords, generals, and emperors for what they were. I can assure you, even the best intentioned can be found to be lacking when measured against the consequences of their choices, or the outcomes of their stands. Still, it's not for me to judge them. Some I have followed of my own free will and even now, I doubt not their righteousness, or their hearts; or even my following them when I did.'

" 'It's as if what they intended was never meant to be, no matter how high and lofty the aspirations. So why raise all the ruckus? Yes, I too have made my mistakes. Abundantly! Now, I stay my hand, serving only the moment, and the righteous instant, keeping my senses honed for the possibility of change. Always waiting and ready, trusting I will know when to move.' "

The Precipice

" 'How do you know what is righteous in the instant?'

" 'The answer to that my brother can only be gotten once you've taken the plunge.'

" 'Plunge?'

" 'Remember the three soldiers. What did you feel when you knew the danger to be certain and imminent? Were you afraid? Was not death staring you in the eye? Had time not stopped? Did you not see your targets as I saw the single field of red on the locust? The precipice my friend. The precipice. Right there to your front. Always! It's a door smack in the middle of your perception. Few ever get so far. Open it! Walk through it! Become fully aware!' "

Bao Ling paused in the narrative, perhaps for effect, then his next words cut through the silence.

"Shen Ling, you need to know this, for your time will come. I will tell you exactly what I told him. I knew in part of what he spoke and said so. As I committed deeper into my own path, changes in perception and awareness began to emerge of their own. At times, the constant voice inside my own head went silent, as though relinquishing the perceived me to the quiet within. Sometimes, unsettled, I'd rush back to the voice, if only to have a tether to the world about me, or perhaps to life itself. The vast quiet seemed ominous in its boundless and unfettered scope. I told him I had become more comfortable lingering in the silence, and found it even more so to my liking than at first, gradually adopting it as a post, staking me to the new essential. Though I still had fear and trepidation with what seemed unknowable, they no longer impeded. It was as though I had nearly come to pronouncing my surface self dead. Gone. Relinquished. I had nothing left to lose, and I felt like a phantom as I moved about. Not quite. I mean I was still of this world, and still there to be seen. But without my endless fears, or my all too evident needs and foibles to exploit against me, those who would harm could not seem to find or lock in on my intentions, or to anticipate and time my movements and responses. It was that way with the three soldiers. They had uniforms, sophisticated weapons and ample body armor. They should have finished me easily. I knew they were thinking that. Yet for them, still not enough. They had great fear, and blatant wants, all glaringly obvious as I stood before them. That's what made them pawns of others. They were stuck, and all too predictable. They weren't born that way, they became that way. To them, I was just another sheep to be shorn, there to suit their whims. Rough me up, strip me of my game, my bow, my arrows, humiliate me, then let the creatures of night suck on my bones.

"When stopped, I freely demonstrated I had nothing of value or of use to them. Surely they would let me pass. So I thought, even hoped, but to no avail. I could see they were from villages much like our own, but had crossed to the other side. Perhaps at first only to survive, but then, in time, they learned from harsh example and mindless repetition to oppress. Could I somehow persuade them back? Was it for me to save their souls? Would they allow me the time and opportunity to do so? The very thought was on the tip of my tongue when I saw the mind of the middle man. He was about to reach for his long-blade and remove my head, certain I could not move or react in those close quarters, outnumbered and pinned there within their midst.

"His miscalculation of course. Grandfather embodied the essence of generations studying the internal energies. Throughout my youth, he had me 'standing like a post' and 'listening.' Sometimes he would seem to ignore me for hours. At first, for me as a young child, it was agonizing. I craved movement and attention. Yet soon enough, the practice became my sanctuary, a place I could go and visit with another me, an inner self, away from the impossibly crowded and hungry world. No, he wasn't ignoring me at all. He taught I came from a family ordained to be the final line against oppression. Whatever that meant. Again, the will of heaven?

"Even then as a child, it seemed to me there was enough oppression going on to work its way around any line, final or not. He said it was in our blood, our past, our future, and could not be changed or ignored, a duty old as time itself. When I boasted to them what he said, my parents grew concerned. They admonished I should humor him, but ignore his eccentricities, explaining for my benefit, 'He is a very old man.' Then they touched their hands to their heads to make sure I understood he was not all there. He was my father's father, and mother feared on my behalf the consequences of his 'rants.' Still, she never contradicted him to his face. Of one thing I am certain. She would have if she believed him wrong. It was her silence on these things which marked all he said to be proper and true, rants or not. Her silence settled it for me!

"He taught I should never strike first. I questioned, 'How is it possible to survive without hitting first?' He laughed, 'It's the only way to survive, threaten no one, ever; but trounce them when attacked.' He carefully added, 'Always listen, read what's there. Inside, center your spirit just like you do when you become a post. If your adversary attacks, it is your right to strike, but then only from the depth of relaxation, where your spirit is integrated and strongest. Like a bolt of lightning, never a laggard. Be committed! They will be frozen in the sticky moment by their ill-considered audacity, and will be very surprised when you turn it back upon them. Be assured, they have never encountered the likes of this! A great hammer indeed! Just drop it on them when they least expect!' A riddle, he repeatedly articulated, always sure to laugh as he did so, doubtless hoping someday a flash of insight would cross my brow. 'Only by doing this will you have certainty in your movement. Certainty is everything! Never forget that! The attacker's hand will stall, befuddled with doubt, and will have no base or root to stand upon. Victory is assured!'

"The three aggressors wore their masks of brazen confidence. The first one thought he had me dead to rights.

No sooner had his hand moved toward his blade, than I pulled three shafts from my pouch and drove the arrows down into his throat with both my hands. He sure didn't plan on that! Luckily, they struck true and punched deep. The others were stunned to see their companion still standing, but frozen, limbs already deadened; blood spurting, quick dead, waiting only to drop. They could have let me be, but instead, broke angles to my left and right as my bow slid from shoulder smoothly to my grip. A maneuver well choreographed to perfection during my time on the run. My next arrow was mounted and the bow drawn as I quick turned left and downed the second. His knife released toward me just as I fired, it seemed I had an eternity to evade its threat. I circled back, turning away from its trajectory and to where I saw the third man easing the draw of his bow to avoid the now errant blade. I remember him cursing under his breath. I sighted on him, setting my third arrow. Just as his eyes returned to me from the wayward blade, I finished him."

The Righteous Instant

"Having said my piece, my attention then returned to Sying Hao. Silence. Recalling the original gist of my interest, and the prudence of shifting topic, he returned again to his 100 pace shot. 'There are other ways to see our targets. Before I first ventured to Southern Mountain, I had known an archer who, to assist my own growth, shared the story of Ah Ju Na[30]. Ah Ju Na was a great prince in an empire to the south. In that world, he came to be known as the greatest of archers. Even in youth, his innate talents were so extraordinary it is said the Supreme Entity manifested to earth in the form of a cousin and lifelong companion to the young prince.'

" 'You mean the Celestial Emperor? I interrupted in disbelief.'

---

[30] Ah Ju Na - Arjuna. The great archer and life companion to the divine Krishna. Arjuna's spiritual dilemma in the midst of battle imminent framed the setting for Krishna's core revelations and teachings as preserved in the Bhagavad Gita.

" 'No. The Celestial Emperor would have had no kind inclination toward Ah Ju Na. The Supreme Entity I speak of is beyond that and emerges from among the deepest roots within the core of all. He, she, or it stands one with Dharma and never deviates from that posture.'

" 'In that instance, the deity manifested as a man, like Ah Ju Na, and knew the young archer would some day play a decisive role in events of cosmic relevance. They were indeed cousins, tied by blood, but more importantly, as friends, they were inseparable. Now limited in his form, and knowing its constraints, the Supreme Entity marveled all the more at his young mate's growing skills and evolution. Having a man's body himself, he knew how difficult it was! Ah Ju Na was born mortal, the same as you and me. You see, once born, we are beyond the hand of the gods. We have free will and that is what shapes how we become. It is a great gift, and allows us to do the impossible, even should the gods oppose. The two companions spent their youths together, and in time the Supreme Entity deemed to serve as charioteer and trusted counselor to his friend. The two were never apart, even when you didn't see them together. Ah Ju Na had many remarkable skills and traits, the greatest always being his genius with the bow. Legend shares with us how his remarkable skill hinged on his ability to see with his mind what reached far beyond his eyes, or the eyes of others.'

" 'Once, while teaching archery to Ah Ju Na and the other princes, Da Rou Na[31], the imperial instructor had them

---

[31] Da Rou Na - "Drona"; supreme teacher of military arts and ethics. Master to Arjuna. Their relationship is fully detailed

draw aim on a falcon in a nearby wood. As bows were set to the ready, the teacher asked each, "Tell me, what do you see?" The first responded, "I see a beautiful field of blue"; of course, he was describing the sky. Another said "white," the clouds. Another, "gray," the feathers; and so on. Then he questioned Ah Ju Na, "What do you see young prince?" Ah Ju Na responded, "I see only black." '

" 'At first puzzled, the teacher asked, "What else besides black?" "Nothing else sir," Ah Ju Na replied, "Just black." The teacher stared toward the target, puzzled. With the others, he could easily figure their focus, but with Ah Ju Na, he was at a loss. His fine eyes could see no black. He turned to Ah Ju Na, "Tell me Prince Ah Ju Na, what specifically are you looking at?" Ah Ju Na replied, "I am staring into the eye of the falcon sir." '

"Sying Hao then clarified, 'So, at 200 paces, did I see the locust or not? Can't answer that, I was looking at his eyes, seeing only rainbows, and relative to them, I knew where his thorax was. The second shot was the more difficult. My awareness of the locust was fine, and filled my consciousness with certainty. Still, as I steadied the shot, I sensed the movement of a hare, saw butterflies fluttering in the between, and a thrush crossed my field of vision angling with the breeze. I felt a gentle rise of wind softly undulating from our rear in the direction of the locust and knew the creature would seek new position when this reached him. I timed my shot when all was reconciled in my aim. I'd say it was a lucky shot, except I can do it all the time. Just like you

---

in the Mahabharata, the timeless Indian classic.

and the three guards, an act of skill which mystifies me still. A talent? A gift?'

"We sat in silence the balance of the evening, watching the stars, contemplating destiny.

"On waking, I found Sying Hao already sitting and staring at the sunrise.

" 'Little Brother, may I beg you accompany me on my journey home? I've seen enough and am content to return to Southern Mountain. We might use the opportunity to sharpen your skills, and to share more thoughts on what two humble souls like us can do, flitting about upon these ripples of circumstance and time.'

" 'That's quite far,' I replied, 'I could be gone the entire season, even longer. Thank you for your kind offer, but this is my home, and here I'm needed. Besides, at heart, I'll always be a lowlander.'

"Sensing my concern regarding the well-being of my compatriots, Sying Hao assured, 'You'd be well served stepping away for now. So too would they. You have become a marked man, even a liability. Already troops scour the villages and outlands looking for the newly proclaimed "Dragon of the Midlands" of whom everyone boasts. The one who had miraculously slain three fully armed soldiers. Or was it 5, perhaps 10, these accounts seem to escalate over time. In fact, as word continues to spread, there's no telling where the tally will stop, especially with someone like you, who has done it more than once, and seems able to replicate the feat at will. For certain though, there are some who do not appreciate your efforts. Bringing you in alive, having some perverted fun, then desecrating your carcass would, for them, portend a bright future. Turning today's salt into tomorrow's honey. What would the example do for your people? The ones you care for? Along with that, you must remember and respect the price extracted from those who protect and supply your needs. Because of you, they too stand at risk, but they don't have your skills or instincts for survival. The warlords will make gruesome examples of them. It has long been the way of usurpers to punish everyone to get at the one.'

"Concerned over what trouble I might bring to Sying Hao, I responded, 'I would not want to burden your journey or your safety with my affairs. If my days be marked or numbered, so be it. I accept it, and will leave the onus to no others. You have no stake in these matters. I bid thee well friend, and consider myself blessed we've had our brief moment together.'

"He answered, 'I'll say this again. You should come with me. It will be better for you, and I expect it will be better for your people to have you gone for a while. You have an opportunity to disappear. I tell you, seize it! Here, you're stuck and can go no further than deeper down. Not to worry over me. I can take care of myself. Together we'll find much to do, and to ponder. Should they come for us, they will not find easy prey with two such as we. Besides, I guarantee the assholes will still be waiting here, praying for the day you return.'

"And so it was. Now seeing clearly into the righteous instant, I packed what little I had, stepping into destiny with my new friend."

Bao Ling
"Stepping into Destiny"

Reflections

In our remaining days together, father made a point of telling me all he could of his time in the western wilderness. He spoke in great detail of his sojourn within the wilds of Southern Mountain, and of the many wonders he beheld. Our own people had already known and spoken of this Southern Mountain. We thought of it as a place on the edge of everything, where empire and civilization ceased and the primal ascended to oust their purpose. A vast quiet in the far west said to be inhabited by ghosts, favored by wizards and mystics, sanctuary to many seekers, refuge to runaways, dropouts, and even deserters, hoping in desperation for a better way. From within emerged an interminable torrent of profound mysteries and unresolved riddles.

He also told of their excursions to the far south, and described a happy people living there, secluded in their tropical paradise. He spoke of abundance, telling of exotic fruits which seemed to grow themselves, and vegetables so plentiful as to require little tending. He told of their art, and their music, and of course their love of verse, sure to add how everything about them seemed as poetry. These same people revered his companion Sying Hao as the adopted son and disciple of the mysteriously disappeared bodhisattva warrior, Sun Wu Kong — who, as Colonel Sun, had mentored Sying Hao from childhood.

Because of Colonel Sun, Sying Hao felt especially obligated to and protective of the Southlanders. By standards in the decimated north, Southlanders had all which everyone needed, and coveted. Jewels could be found in the sandy beds of their streams and even the most ordinary among them took to adorning themselves with gold and silver trinkets which seemed to give them glow as they moved about in the daylight.

I asked what might be the connection between Sun Wu Kong and the Southlanders? Father answered that according to Sying Hao, Sun lived among them for a time, purposefully studying their many collections of Sutras, and then intently engaging their meditative standards and practices. Sying Hao further shared with father how Sun acknowledged achieving his grand awareness while living and communing among the Southlanders. They reminded him of his own kind, or so he said. But that story will be for another time.

Because of their ample blessings, and what others felt to be their seeming weakness (tolerance and compassion are sometimes read that way), they were branded as ripe for plucking. Those in the north have a history of taking what they want, and assimilating whatever it is they feel they need. Until that particular time, the Southland had been spared intrusions from the outside. The combination of mountains, wild rivers, oppressive heat, venomous creatures, and mysterious illnesses had in the past been enough to protect them.

Only stark necessity, mounted upon generations of chaos and conflict could re-fire Northerners' motivations to overcome such known and daunting obstacles. Being ever mindful of the Southlanders, and the growing threat of exposure to the ravages of northern avarice, Sying Hao took it upon himself to honor Colonel Sun's sworn oath to ensure their independence, safety and freedom.

Father also related his escapades while in the north and west, for a time partnering with the Shu tribes in their own struggle for survival. This led to his eventual return to the roiling heart of the once supreme but now hopelessly embattled empire, where he came into his own and proved pivotal in all which followed. Preserved in the words and recitations of master poet Zhi Mei, his deeds have become legendary. He often clarified for my benefit: "Some things, though difficult and trying, are just meant to be. Looking back, it seems all so clear; direct and easy in its natural order. But going forward into and through all of it tried one's soul with endless uncertainty, and the unknowable. I had no choice but to come to intimate terms with fear, and then, ultimately, profound loss. Every day spent fending against such torrents could seem a lifetime anywhere else. Yet here I am. In a way, I've become ageless, marked by the hard temper of my experiences."

He explained how, because of those trials, he felt as though he had passed through many existences, many cycles, and many worlds ... then smiled when he concluded with, " — and yet, against all odds, somehow managed to survive, in the end returning to my people and our home. Your home. Even Sun Wu Kong couldn't achieve that for himself. And now I can look back over everything and see this newest challenge to be just another strand remaining from the original purpose. Long ago, Grandfather had spoken only truth and told me all I needed to know, but I couldn't see it then, at least not in the magnitude of the undertaking. We are indeed a family anointed to be the final line against oppression. The will of heaven has nothing to do with it. I remain bound … so long as I live."

Though he didn't say it directly to me, when he turned his eyes my way, I knew. For better or worse, I too had been bound.

The tales and legends emanating from those times leave no uncertainty on one point. The road to peace and normalcy for each and all of them demanded great sacrifice, loneliness, unending trials, and a tortuous uncertain path with no promised end. With weighted heart, father would recite for me the names of comrades who fell. He had shaped the memory of their deeds into verse, a poetic litany of infinite melancholy and sadness, recalling why and how each had left his or her indelible mark on what followed. I've no doubt he wanted me to hear his own words, his testament, and what he carried within because of it, the living truth of it — not the legends, and in that, I would better know him, and myself.

Now my friends, following the example of my father, the time has come for me too to move along, and for you to simply take in the tales which I promise will eventually unfold.

Who can say where they will lead you? Who can say where you will end? Are we so different from one another? In your own worlds, do you not also share the fates of heroes?

Does it not seem like magic of a kind?

Acknowledgments

Once again, Bobbi Youtcheff came up with an image for the cover which spoke to the themes at hand. The original photograph was titled, "Fall at Point Defiance." Point Defiance is a mammoth park within Tacoma, abutting the Puget Sound. Inside the sanctuary, one can glimpse remnants of old growth forests, framed by wondrous displays of wildlife. Bald eagles circle overhead, sea lions can be heard in the distance, orcas can be sighted in the sound, raccoons brazenly molest the hikers. One splendid autumn day, Bobbi found an ancient oak, its leaves wildly ablaze in the golden sunlight. That became her focus, and her subject. She shared the image with me, and I knew instantly it would be a book cover. Only I had not yet written the book which would justify its use, at least not until now. What you see on our cover has been re-worked and cropped, then turned sideways with shadings enhanced and intensified. We end up with a visual metaphor for complexity, challenge, chaos, turmoil and change, all rooted in the infinite organic complexity of the original image. A remnant of old growth, one of few remaining, as metaphor for the eventualities of life, and its many uncertainties, as well as for hope and survival.

On a different note, creating a work of fiction can be a daunting experience. First, there is the work itself, then the endless re-writes, the editing, touch ups and fine tuning; and finally the layout, now necessitated twice, once for E-Book, once for hard copy. Of course, all the while, life beckons, crises arise, and innumerable pirate thieves of time threaten to seize every dedicated moment.

There is however, one effective counter, without which nothing would ever arrive at the point of final
fruition ... having a dedicated editor.

That role has again been voluntarily and unsparingly filled by my friend and fellow explorer of life's mysteries, Bryan Smith. Bryan is a retired professor of mathematics and computer science (Professor Emeritus, University of Puget Sound), who on learning I was a writer, offered his expert services to edit and opine on anything I planned to publish.

At first I hesitated, I had been down the path before, and often as not, it proved to be an exercise in diversion.

But I must say, from the very first, Professor Bryan attacked (I mean that in a positive sense) whatever I tendered with a ruthless, yet fair-minded commitment targeting excellence, clarity, polish, and pertinence.

Thank you Bryan. I couldn't have done it without you. Well, hold that thought. Maybe I could have, but it would have taken ten years longer. Recognizing your efforts and profound contribution, I must freely acknowledge, if only to spare you any guilt, the mistakes and oversights are all mine.

The artwork you find within was done by Renee Knarreborg. Renee and I had collaborated on a number of projects over the years, when life intervened and we went our own ways, submitting to the demands of professions and caring for families. We lost contact for quite some time, mostly my fault. When I felt the current stories needed visuals to reinforce characterizations, I knew precisely who would be best for the task. I re-contacted Renee, tested the waters to see if she was interested, and consider myself blessed and fortunate that she jumped immediately on board. When she wasn't attending to regional power and utility issues, or running audits, she somehow found the time to take in my story lines and convoluted character sketches, to come up with the final images which grace these pages. As always, she kept it simple, often pencil or ink on paper, running through many iterations until the images and depictions aligned.

I am also indebted to the many masters who have befriended me over the years and who took great care sharing their knowledge and remarkable skills with this stumbling pilgrim. Foremost among them, the incomparable Isidro Archibeque, whose teachings and exploits I have attempted to document and preserve at:

www.ironcrane.com

Lest any others be unintentionally overlooked, my complete lineage can be viewed at:

http://www.ironcrane.com/IC_Flowchart_Color.jpeg

About the Author

Billy Ironcrane is the writing and music performing pseudonym for Bill Mc Cabe, a lifelong explorer of life's experiences and unending surprises. Raised in inner city Philadelphia during the 1950's and 60's, he partook in the revolutionary currents of change, protest, activism, and idealism which characterized the era. While a teen, he spent summers on the Jersey coast hawking newspapers, tossing burgers and exploring places like Wildwood and Atlantic City where he encountered flea circuses, Gene Krupa hanging between sets at the Steel Pier, petrified mermaids and the fabulously wealthy promenading the boardwalk at night flashing mink stoles, diamonds, tuxes and studded canes. Atlantic City dubbed itself, "The World's Playground." All the stuff of dreams as he returned to some flop house where he slept for ten bucks a week, sharing occasional space with Polish immigrants working the summer trade, and the ever present army of cats.

He departed the inner city still in his teens, and pushed blindly into the unknown never to return, sensing to be static and do nothing would be terminal, as in fact it proved to be for many of his mates. In the decades following, he pursued new awarenesses, swam exotic currents, trekked remote tropical forests, became a soldier, ambled southwest deserts at night, slept through thunderstorms alongside petrified forests, trekked the Rockies, mastered the martial arts, jogged with blacktail deer in hills surrounding Monterey, explored Zen, motorcycled the California coast, scaled Pfeiffer Rock, freelanced, traversed the Cascades, slept beneath ancient redwoods in remote Los Padres, joined the corporate jungle, raised a family, helped birth a medical corporation, then hung up a shingle and lived on wits and ingenuity until the muse of the 60's again tapped his shoulder, ordering, "Time to shift gears, Billy."

His journey to self actualize is chronicled at www.ironcrane.com. His commitment to roots music and preserving threads of tradition can be found at www.bluemuse.org.

Characters and Incidentals

Bao Ling - "The Dragon of the Midlands." Protagonist around whom many of our stories revolve. Master archer, outlaw, peasant, farmer, healer, wanderer, revolutionary, and in the end, a father. In some ways, he is everyman … trying to make sense of the unknowable and the uncertain, while preserving his connection to the simple life of his forbears, and to the ways of the land he loves.

Cao Cao - (155 - 15 March 220 CE). King of and then posthumously declared Emperor of Wei. Ambitious and talented general who sought to harness the Will of Heaven and establish a new empire, intending to succeed the failed Han. A talented leader, warrior, strategist, and scholar, as well as a renowned poet. Remarkably loyal to his friends and allies, he was equally regarded as ruthless, cruel and merciless in securing his objectives. History tells us he succeeded to a considerable degree, and his empire is remembered as the "Cao Wei" not to be confused with lesser successors, also named Wei. It lasted less than half a century, a mere blip in the roll of dynasties. His doings unfolded long before the events of our stories, but were factors nonetheless.

What remained after his demise rapidly descended into chaos. Suffering beset the land for generations. The "Wei" alluded to in these accounts are a mere shadow of the original "Cao Wei." No more than a specter of what once was, but still vying for control of the land, scrounging every which where to replenish resources depleted by successive generations of war machines foolishly unleashed. Therein lies the significance and relevance of once forgotten places like Ling village, and the Shu mountain passes.

Colonel Sun (Sun Wu Kong) - Honored officer and counselor in the service of Liu Bei. Close comrade to Zhuge Liang, and colleague to Guan Yu. Mentor and fatherly influence to Sying Hao. Possibly an immortal, possibly a descendant of a different species. Forever shrouded in mystery, except for the lingering monuments of his deeds, demeanor, and awe inspiring presence. Directly, or indirectly, his influence and spirit can be felt throughout our tales.

Dragon Bow - The incomparable bow of Sun Wu Kong. Recognized by those who knew of it to represent perfection of the bowyer's craft. Believed by witnesses of its power to be divine in origin. While simple in appearance, close inspection showed it to be complex in every detail, designed so its very core resonated with and drew strength from the character of its holder. One unworthy could scarcely draw the cord, let alone use it. Supreme in its authority, it came to be known as the "Hundred Li Bow." In the hands of one with righteous character, and the requisite degree of skill, there seemed no end to its tactical reach. Through Sying Hao, it found its way into the hands of Bao Ling, who casually referred to it as "One-Li." Perhaps he preferred not to draw undue attention to its potential.

Fa Miu - "Old Fox." He is a character appearing in several of our tales. A practical, gifted, and worldly wise gentleman, he often appears at first to be slave to whatever system or scheme he serves, yet somehow always manages to function independently with his hands subtly on the helm. Truth be told, his true nature is excellence, and his aim inevitably directed toward the common good. We learn of him in another tale, as the elder of two toll collectors encountered by Bao Ling on entering Fortune's Gateway. At first glance, a fox faced, world-wise and very clever old man, seemingly relegated to obscurity, bemoaning his fate. Still, he makes a lasting impression on the young archer. Acting as toll collector, Fa Miu takes special interest in Bao Ling and his lady companion Zhi Mei. On hearing the current account of Master Li Confronting the Wei, Bao Ling learns considerably more about the stranger he luckily encountered, albeit by chance.

Fortune's Gateway - A major trade center on the western end of the Shu mountain ranges, backed by the great western wilderness, an endless expanse, and what remained of the defunct Silk Road which had long before proven so beneficial to the Han Dynasty. Despite the collapse of Han, and afterward, the collapse of the Shu Han (the western empire headed by Liu Bei), Fortune's Gateway proved very much to be deserving of its name. There, one found a lineage of traders who prospered by treating all parties as equals, so long as they had something to transact, and needed something in return. Foremost among those parties were the Shu people of the mountains, long oppressed, and forever contending with invaders from the east. Being practical, many in Fortune's Gateway recognized the continuing benefit of their association with the Shu. So long as the mountain tribes fended off those in the east, Fortune's Gateway remained for all practical purposes, autonomous. They had flourished under Liu Bei, and at the time of our first story, still remained insulated from upheavals in the east, thanks to the resistance of the Shu mountain tribes.

Guan Yu - (160-220 CE). Also referred to as Guan Gung, Lord Guan, or simply Guan. Sworn brother to Liu Bei and Zhang Fei (bound three as one by their Peach Garden Oath). Virtually peerless among human warriors. Revered as a staunch patron of righteousness. Protector of the oppressed, guardian of the weak and vulnerable. In the lineage of our accounts, he becomes companion and peer to Sun Wu Kong (Colonel Sun). He is the only human ever considered by Sun Wu Kong to be his martial equal. In his prime, with no more than his Green Dragon Blade in hand, Guan Yu could by himself, stand down an entire enemy army.

He Ling - Paternal Grandfather to Bao Ling. Of considerable influence in shaping his character and developing his unique talents. Though little is said of him here, in time he will be shown connected to a history of mysterious influences which only become apparent to Bao Ling as his own journey into uncertainty and challenge begins.

Iron Hand Gao - Friend of He Ling. Martial and life tutor to the child Bao Ling. He is mentioned only in a passing reference. Though their time together had been short due to harsh necessity, the impact of his character on Bao Ling had been profound. Once one knew a man like Iron Hand Gao, he would fear no other.

Jin Dynasty - (265-420 CE). War of the Eight Princes. The period leading up to and enveloping our stories.

Knights of Wei - The supreme warriors of the Wei Empire. Bred by hard trial and constant challenge, then endowed with the full support of the state and transformed by the highest and most sophisticated metaphysical arts and sciences into the most formidable killing machines ever devised. Their feats and accomplishments became legendary and were heralded throughout the land. They were even likewise grudgingly recognized by their enemies. The imperial court took great care to orchestrate a formal code of chivalry and morality surrounding these killing machines, citing them as the high standard to which all good citizens should aspire. Their enemies of course, knew far better. The Knights of Wei were no less than the unleashed hounds of Yama, as capable of unforgivable atrocities as any man turned demon. The five in our story are the pick of the crop, the most feared in the land.

Liang San - Town head (mayor) of Fortune's Gateway when Li Fung issues his challenge to the Knights of Wei. A rarity for the time, selected by the people he governed, and not appointed by the royal court or regional authority. His constant love, hate relationship with Fa Miu, his right hand man is evident throughout our account. He holds loyalty to only three things. Fortune's Gateway, himself, and, depending on his mood, Fa Miu.

Li Fung - "Master Li" of the Mountain People. Village elder. Martial master. He figures prominently in the personal development of Shi-Hui Ke, both as child, and as man. The first story speaks much of him, and for now, we'll say no more.

Liu Bei - (unknown 161 – 10 June 223 CE). The incomparable man of righteousness, and distant relation to the Han emperor. A sandal maker who rose to prominence as a formidable military commander, and because of his unsparing dedication to restoration of the Han Dynasty. Retreating to save what remained of his forces, he founded the Shu Han empire in the remote west, and prospered beyond all expectations, his achievements the stuff of dreams and legends. Until his demise, he remained a key principal during the period of the Three Kingdoms. He felt the Shu tribes to be a most noble and honorable people, believing that so long as they remained viable, there would be no direct path for Cao Cao and Wei to attack from the east. To that end, he ensured the Shu remained independent, and always, a respected ally.

Long Hsieh - Wei minister who agrees to the challenge tendered by Li Fung, setting up the match between Li Fung, and the feared Knights of Wei. As representative of the empire, he had been sent to secure the loyalty of Fortune's Gateway to the imperial eastern court, and thus sever the western logistical lines supporting the resistance of the Shu tribes. The story unfolds as he seeks to weave his spell with promises of unprecedented riches to the gathered townsfolk.

Shi-Hui Ke - One of the Shu Mountain people. Abbot of Crystal Springs temple, a mysterious preserve and one of several fortresses meticulously conceived by Zhuge Liang to secure the Shu Roads from invasion; and to protect, as per Liu Bei's directive, the culture and heritage of the mountain people. Although a monk and man of peace, Shi-Hui Ke remains an ardent patriot, and has found purpose in his role as defender of his people and their ways. In his youth, he had attained renown as a singularly gifted martial artist, particularly in archery, before losing his left arm midway from the shoulder resulting from unlucky encounter with a sadistic band of Wei mercenaries. They cut off his left thumb, assuring he could wield no bow. Gangrene set in and the arm could not be saved. In some ways, the unfortunate loss of his arm proved a blessing … in time, the once consummate archer, now monk, found within his higher states of awareness, the secret of the "thought arrow." Bao Ling had already seen Abbot Hui's remarkable skill, projecting nothing but concentrated thought to strike and deter a stalking tiger. The full account is presented elsewhere. He also appears to have gained privy to the alchemy of longevity, or so concludes Bao Ling, but that is a different story.

Shu-Ting tribe - The displaced mountain people residing in the environs surrounding Crystal Springs. A collection of Shu tribespersons, looking to reform and restore their culture. This branch of the Shu had a long history of dealings with those in Fortune's Gateway, and over time, the two groups became respectfully interdependent.

Sying Hao - Mentor to Bao Ling. A onetime war orphan who became apprentice and adopted son to Sun Wu Kong. Friend of the Southlanders; archer supreme, master of the transformations; able to project consciousness, and to move about without detection; scholar of the classics, a bow craftsman of singular caliber. Sometimes called "Fenghua Yan" (weathered rock), or "The Man from Southern Mountain."

Yama - "King Yama". A devil of sorts; or perhaps what we might think of as the incarnation of death. Presides over hell and is accountable for the life, death and transmigration of human souls. Keeps true the final ledger and ensures his fearsome legions bring the newly departed to their end judgment. Relishes chaos and induces strife. Truly enjoys his job, particularly the part where he gets to torment those deserving. Once, when confronted by the Creator for his evil doings, he defended himself most eloquently, arguing to the Creator, "Hey … isn't this my job? Did you make me for any other purpose? Can you think of anyone who can do it better than me? Forgive me sire, but I fail to see where there is a problem." His logic and integrity, thus convinced the Creator. He justly earned his release and was freed to go about his business unimpeded.

Zhang Fei - (unknown - died 221 CE). Sworn brother to Guan Yu and Liu Bei. Also a singular warrior, one whom Guan Yu deemed his peer and often boasted of. Known for his uncontrollable temper, it proved to be his ultimate undoing, said to have been assassinated by his own men, but not until fulfilling a life of epic feats and undeniable heroism.

Zhi Mei - A farm girl whose family (father and brother) were killed by Wei marauders. She had been kidnapped and abused until stumbled upon and rescued by Bao Ling,